PRAISE FOR JULIANA BRANDT'S
THE WOLF OF CAPE FEN

"A stunning seaside fairy tale that will absorb readers until the very end."

—*Booklist*

"A mesmerizing piece of magical realism packed with mystery, suspense, and, most important, love."

—*School Library Journal*

"This intriguing mystery culminates in a startling, literally transforming climax."

—*Kirkus Reviews*

"Debut author Brandt's atmospheric, genre-bending middle-grade novel brings grim fairy-tale magic to a small peninsular town in the early twentieth century."

—*Publishers Weekly*

"Liza's story weaves its magic around you, as wild and wondrous as the dreams at the book's heart. Cape Fen and its inhabitants will haunt you long after the book is closed."

—Cindy Baldwin, author of *Where the Watermelons Grow*

"A hauntingly gorgeous fable full of lofty dreams, terrible bargains, and accepting who you are. Cape Fen's secrets and magic had me enthralled from the start, and the conclusion to this dark and wondrous tale will stick with me forever."

—Sean Easley, author of the Hotel Between series

"An atmospheric, mysterious tale of magic, community, and the true meaning of family, *The Wolf of Cape Fen* is a gorgeous debut that will hook its readers from the first page."

—Diane Magras, author of *The Mad Wolf's Daughter*

"The sisters' relationship forms the backbone of the story, and readers will share Eliza's frustration at adult obfuscation and enjoy her satisfyingly clever bargaining skills, resulting in a story that would be a good choice for fans of Anne Ursu. Softly spangled black-and-white chapter title illustrations preface brief dream interludes belonging to other Fenians, emphasizing that the whole community is bound up in the baron's magic and helping to harmonize the novel's contrasting moods of coastal-town hominess and stark unease."

—*Bulletin of the Center for Children's Books*

ALSO BY JULIANA BRANDT

The Wolf of Cape Fen

A Wilder Magic

JULIANA BRANDT

sourcebooks
young readers

Published by Sourcebooks Young Readers, an imprint of Sourcebooks Kids
P.O. Box 4410, Naperville, Illinois 60567-4410
(630) 961-3900
sourcebookskids.com
Library of Congress Cataloging-in-Publication Data

Names: Brandt, Juliana, author.
Title: A wilder magic / Juliana Brandt.
Description: Naperville, Illinois : Sourcebooks Young Readers, [2021] |
    Audience: Grades 4-6. | Summary: "For generations, Sybaline Shaw's
    family has lived in an enchanted valley in the Appalachian Mountains,
    using their magic to help grow the land. But now the government has
    built a dam that will force the Shaws to relocate, and they're running
    out of time before their home will be flooded"-- Provided by publisher.
Identifiers: LCCN 2020048053 (print) | LCCN 2020048054 (ebook)
Subjects: CYAC: Magic--Fiction. | Home--Fiction. | Families--Fiction. |
    Appalachian Region--Fiction.
Classification: LCC PZ7.1.B75152 Wi 2021 (print) | LCC PZ7.1.B75152
    (ebook) | DDC [Fic]--dc23
LC record available at https://lccn.loc.gov/2020048053
LC ebook record available at https://lccn.loc.gov/2020048054

Source of Production: Sheridan Books, Chelsea, Michigan, United States
Date of Production: March 2021
Run Number: 5020753

Printed and bound in the United States of America.
SB 10 9 8 7 6 5 4 3 2 1

Mary Parton,

you lent me your strength and your wisdom,

and you showed me the heart of Appalachia.

Thank you.

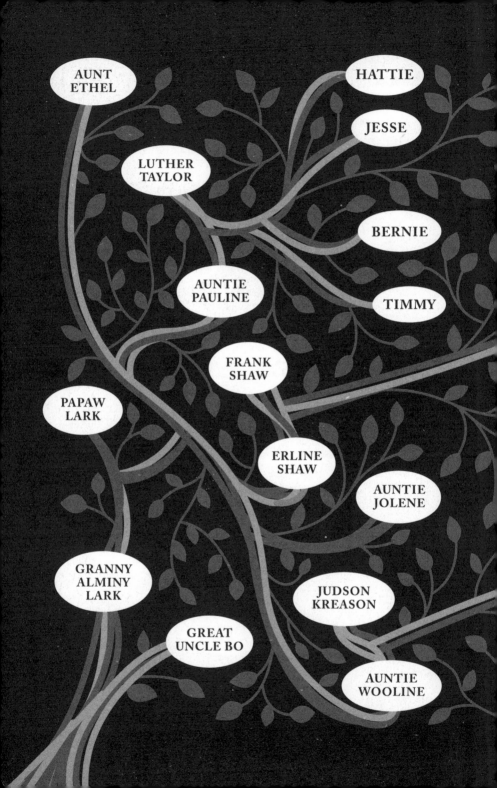

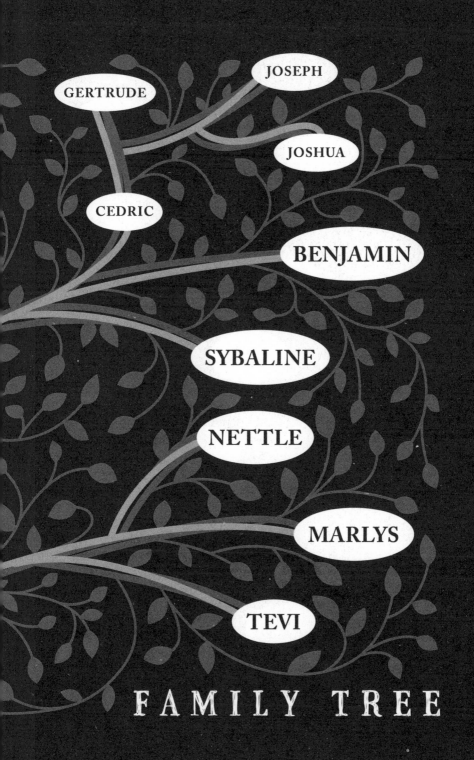

GERTRUDE

JOSEPH

JOSHUA

CEDRIC

BENJAMIN

SYBALINE

NETTLE

MARLYS

TEVI

FAMILY TREE

CHAPTER 1

The valleys in Appalachia were all dressed for an outing.

Red pom-pom frocks and green needle suits draped over the trees. Strands of ribbon vines hugged their necks. Shoes of crimson and orange leaves clung to their feet. The valleys and surrounding mountains were glimmering, and they were dressed to the nines, but that did not describe the valley in which Sybaline Shaw lived. The valley in which Sybaline Shaw lived made all those *other* valleys shed their leaves and tuck themselves into bed for the winter, ashamed they hadn't shown up to the autumn party in even finer dress.

Her valley was more than glimmering. It was *magical*.

The warmth of her mountains filled her to the brim as she sat at her kitchen table and ground corn with her handheld mill. She stared out the open front door. Smoke crept between the boughs, a haze that hung along the horizon. Past that, the sun rose high over the eastern side of the valley, spotlighting the quilted mountains in a blur of light.

The handle of the mill slipped against the calluses on Sybaline's hand. She wiped her palm on her smock and blew on it, drying the sweat on her skin, before grabbing up the spinning handle again. Inside the mill, corn fell through the funnel and into the grinder below. Fresh cornmeal piled into a bowl that she would later cook into flapjacks and cornbread.

Her mother came up the front steps of the porch. Magic warmed in the air and tightened the feeling of the world, as if a lightning storm were about to pass through the valley. Momma'd likely been using the magic to help grow vegetables in the garden: pumpkins, carrots, collard greens. A wide basket filled her arms, piled high with corn. She paused in the threshold, arms tense around the basket.

"Momma?" Sybaline kept turning the mill.

A secret expression crossed Momma's face. Dark hair clung to the perspiration on her neck, sticking to a deep wrinkle in her skin.

"*Momma?*" Sybaline asked.

Momma took a hesitant step into the room, finally saying, "I thought you were sitting in your father's chair."

Sybaline stopped churning, shocked. "I would never."

"I don't know what I was thinking." Momma set the basket on the table and pressed a kiss with one hand to the air above Poppa's chair. It had sat empty for two years, untouched since the moment he'd stood and walked out the door, answering the summons of the government to go to war.

Sybaline pushed hard on the crank and forced her thoughts away from Poppa and the letter they'd received from him recently. *I'm doing just fine, saw a robin the other day*, he'd written.

"Wooline stopped by while I was gardening. She invited us to a fish fry tonight, and she needs you to go fetch your cousins. She wants them home," Momma said.

"Auntie Wooline always makes me go get them," Sybaline complained, shoving hard against the churn.

"Which means you shouldn't be surprised she's asking you now. Your cousins listen to you."

"They listen to me, because I tell them if they don't, then Auntie Wooline will come for them, and if Auntie Wooline has to drop her work to get them, they'll regret it."

Momma barked out a laugh. "You're their last warning. Better for them that they know it."

Sybaline hated leaving a task unfinished, but still, she unhooked the grinder from where it was clamped to the edge of the table. She put it in its proper place, then stepped into the world outside, with its sun-warmed sky and tender-feathered breeze.

The valley enveloped her, mountains rising in every

direction, their leaves stained a hundred different shades of red, orange, yellow, and purple. The pincushion clouds hovering at their tops were stuck through with wheeling birds.

She headed into the backyard, where endless rows of trees climbed the side of the mountain that towered behind their house. Under their shade, she wiggled her bare toes in the crunchy leaves, finding soft moss hidden beneath. The insides of her body tingled. This was how magic felt, alive and syrupy and warm inside her, almost as if she'd eaten and was full to the brim with good food and happiness.

The magic sparked in her fingertips, and in response, the woods bent toward her. The magic existed in the land, a piece of nature itself. It appeared as a slight dancing of the branches, twigs shivering at her proximity and leaves spinning toward her head. She raised her hands and twirled in the rainbow confetti, laughing loose the tension that had tightened the muscles in her chest while talking with Momma about Poppa.

Momma. Sybaline dropped her hands and the branches snapped back into place, quivering as if a breeze wafted by instead of Sybaline's pull on the magic. She was too responsible to play with the magic like this, and if Momma were here, she would remind her of that fact.

Before Poppa had left for war, he'd told Sybaline it was her job to be exactly as dutiful as Momma needed, which was perfectly dutiful at all times. With both her older brothers moved away, it was up to her to take care of home.

Somber now, Sybaline continued toward the creek that ran through their land and met up with Auntie Wooline's. If they weren't busy with chores, her cousins could usually be found playing games in the stream. The trickling of water came through the forest. She headed toward it and popped out of the path, finding herself on the bank of a small, but swift, creek. Upstream, the water began at a natural spring that was Sybaline's family's water source.

Magic tingled against her bare feet. It told her that someone was using it, and it certainly wasn't her.

It had to be her cousins.

"Where are you?" she asked.

A giggle came from her right, but when Sybaline looked, all she saw was water and stones and woods and leaves and a cluster of vines hanging from a tree limb.

And then, because she knew exactly how to make her cousins do as she wanted, she said, "*Get*," in her most stern and no-nonsense voice.

Magic warmed the air before her, pushing and pulling at the pieces of nature. Then, water whooshed, making a mini-waterfall that fell in a rush into the creek. Marlys appeared near the right bank, in all her wild-haired glory, and from across the creek, Tevi appeared as well, a small replica of her older sister.

"You're no fun," Marlys said. With magic, she pushed at the last bits of water that clung to her dress, forcing it away from her and into the creek until she was dry.

"You're the opposite of fun," Tevi echoed, trying to do the same as her sister, but of course, her control of magic wasn't as refined, leaving her dress good and damp along the hem.

"I'm plenty of fun, just not when your momma's waiting for you and my momma's waiting for me," Sybaline said, then asked, "Where's Nettle?"

"Dunno," Marlys shrugged.

"Dunno," Tevi said, gaze skittering toward the hanging vine and back to the river, as if she wanted very much to stare at it but knew she shouldn't. It was much the same way she played Old Maid, trying hard not to give away her hand and giving it away all the same.

"You're not very good at camouflage," Sybaline said, looking straight at the vines.

Nettle released the magic that held the vines in a clump around her body. "You wouldn't have known if Tevi hadn't given away my spot."

"I didn't give you away!" Tevi stomped a foot. "I didn't give anyone away."

"You gave *us* away. You're the one who giggled," Marlys pointed out.

Tevi hunched her shoulders and then launched herself across the creek and tackled Marlys into the water.

Nettle joined Sybaline on the bank. She was four weeks younger than Sybaline, and four inches shorter. Her short stature did nothing to hide the energy that vibrated inside her though. She was always the one to propose ideas that would get them into trouble, and Sybaline was left with the task of talking her out of her terrible plans.

Sybaline turned to head down the path. "Y'all are using magic wrong, you know. You shouldn't use magic for—"

"Unnatural reasons. I know, I know, Sybaline. You sound like my momma," Nettle interrupted. *"Don't use magic in ways contrary to the natural world; it'll turn you into a tree as a consequence,* she says."

"I've used magic plenty in all sorts of ways, and I've still never turned into an actual tree," Marlys said as she climbed out of the creek, leaving Tevi behind.

"Yet," said Nettle. "Besides, you wouldn't turn into a tree. You'd turn into a pigweed."

"Would not! I'd be a laurel tree. Something pretty."

"Pretty *and* common." Nettle pointed at a host of laurel bushes only five paces away.

"Common's better than gross, which is what you'd be. You'd be poison oak!"

Nettle swatted at Marlys, who jumped back with a laugh. She grabbed up a stick she'd stuck into the bank and pulled out a stringer from the creek. A line of fish dangled from its end. "We're having a fish fry tonight. I was supposed to run by your house this morning and invite you. S'pose I'm inviting you now."

"You're too late. Your momma came by and invited us herself," Sybaline said.

"I'm going to be in trouble, aren't I?"

"Probably."

Nettle sighed, though she didn't look all that disappointed. She never stayed unhappy long, no matter what the problem was, not like Sybaline who couldn't ever rid her head of bad news.

Marlys and Tevi barreled down the path, nearly tripping Nettle. They were all mirror images of one another, just different heights, like the steps of stairs. Sybaline looked enough like them that most people knew on sight they were related. They had the same dark eyes, pale skin that burned during the summer, and wispy hair that fell loose from braids by midday.

"Are you coming to the fish fry tonight, Sybaline?" Marlys asked.

"I like fish," Tevi said. "Except…I don't like it when I eat it too fast, because then it makes me puke."

"If you eat anything too fast, you puke," Marlys said. "And you always eat too fast, which means you always puke. You've spent seven years puking."

"Have not!" Tevi said.

"You used to puke up milk when you were a baby."

Tevi growled, but Nettle snapped out a hand and grabbed up the back of her dress before she could tackle Marlys again.

The path ended at the cleared field that surrounded Sybaline's house on three sides. They'd come out on the southern side, and from there, Sybaline had a good view of their front porch. This time, it was Sybaline who reached out and grabbed someone. She didn't really pay attention to who, just so long as she stopped the entire group from blundering into the field where anyone would be able to see them.

Momma stood in the doorway, elbows jutting out and body taking up as much space as possible. Auntie Wooline was there. So was Auntie Pauline, Auntie Jolene, and… Sybaline's jaw dropped. There was Aunt Ethel walking through the eastern edge of the field, looking for all the world like a giant ready to wreak havoc on whoever had disturbed her rest. Aunt Ethel was always the one people wanted on their side if a fight was about to go down.

Sybaline's momma had four sisters, and if *all* the Lark sisters were gathered and it wasn't dinnertime, it meant something big concerning the family had happened.

"Is that a stranger?" asked Marlys.

Sybaline squinted and saw that indeed, among all her aunts, a stubby man wearing a floppy hat stood with his shoulders hunched in a way that made him look as if he were very overwhelmed.

Tevi said, "When I grow up, I want to be a stranger."

"A stranger isn't a *job*, dummy," Marlys said.

"Shh," Sybaline said.

"I could be a stranger if I wanted," Tevi said.

"I said *shush*!" Sybaline bit out fast, her teeth clenched. Tevi looked at her with rounded eyes. "I know that man."

It was a stranger who wasn't a stranger.

A stranger Sybaline had met once before.

A stranger who had come to take them away from the valley.

CHAPTER 2

"*Go hide*," Sybaline said.

Marlys took one look at Sybaline's fierce expression, then grasped Tevi's hand. Fast as mice scurrying away from a hawk, they disappeared into the woods without a trace.

"You remember him, don't you?" Sybaline asked.

"I couldn't forget if I tried," Nettle said, grim-faced.

The man on the porch was an official from the Tennessee Valley Authority. They made dams throughout the mountains to control flooding and make electricity. Too bad making those dams meant families—families like Sybaline's—couldn't live in the valleys anymore.

She dug up the memory from years before: the TVA official clasping papers in his hands, Sybaline sitting before the fireplace with one of her brothers, Momma with her arms covered in dirt from the garden, Poppa standing in the doorway and protecting them from the news the man brought.

"Last time he came was right before your daddy left," Nettle said.

"Don't say it like that." Sybaline stared harder at her house, blinking fast to clear away the pricks of tears that stung her eyes. Saying Poppa *left* made it sound like he'd had a choice.

Nettle's own daddy had been injured working at their gristmill years ago and hadn't been taken in the war because of it. She wound her fingers around Sybaline's. "Your daddy didn't complain about going, Syb. He's proud to be a soldier. I know you're scared, but he wants to help win the war."

"I'm not scared." She refused to be scared. Being scared meant there was a chance he wouldn't come home.

Nettle started sneaking forward.

Sybaline held tight to her hand and pulled, jerking her to a halt. "Where are you going?"

"I was planning on eavesdropping."

"You'll get caught."

"*We'll* get caught. You're coming with me."

Sybaline released Nettle, as if her skin burned. "Oh no. No, I'm not. I'm not a snoop, and I'm not going to make Momma mad."

"You might not be a snoop, but I am." Nettle's feet *shush*ed over the leaves, a slow pace that someone might could mistake for a deer.

The woods turned quiet and watchful, everything around her holding its breath to see what Sybaline would do. It didn't take her long to decide—she couldn't let her cousin step into a mistake. She needed to be beside her to save her, if need be.

The forest was cleared out around their home, leaving wide-open space for Momma's garden. On the back side, trees grew tall and blocked the heat of the sun. Both girls walked heel-to-toe through the woods, as soundless as they could, and approached the rear of the house.

Sybaline gripped the edge of a windowsill and peered into the back bedroom, crossing her fingers that Momma had left the bedroom door open to let air flow throughout the house. Momma had, and because of it, she could see straight through the bedroom and kitchen to the front porch beyond.

"They're all here," Nettle whispered. "Even Aunt Ethel. That's bad."

"It's real bad." Sybaline set her ear to the window, but she couldn't hear through the glass. She itched inside, as if her anger at not knowing what they were talking about was growing under her skin and wanted to get out.

"Desperate times, Sybaline."

Scratching at her arm and the strange way her body had turned hot with anger, she said, "Call for desperate measures."

Nettle crouched low and led the way.

Around they went until they came to the porch. The porch itself was hollow underneath and wrapped 'round with the boards. It didn't used to have siding. If it still didn't, the girls could've hidden beneath it, but Poppa had boarded it up before leaving to keep wild animals from making homes beneath there. The aunts were talking too quiet; their voices were muffled. Sybaline needed to be on the front side of the house to hear what was being said, but if she went up there, their aunts would shoo them away.

"Now what?" Sybaline said.

Nettle looked at her as if she were stupid. Magic heated around her. Leaves slid along the ground, as if propelled by a swift wind, and collected around Nettle, turning her into a leaf pile instead of a girl.

"That's not how magic's supposed to be used!" Sybaline hissed.

"Desperate times," Nettle whispered from the middle of the pile, and then crawled away from Sybaline and toward the front porch.

Momma had told her all the stories in the family of people who'd forced the magic down unnatural paths. Magic should only be used in ways the natural world already worked: to help plants thrive, to encourage growth, to turn the underbrush verdant and lush. Anything that didn't help the valley flourish could get a person turned full-magic in consequence. They'd disappear into the woods, never to be seen again...at least not as human.

It'd happened with her papaw. Momma said that after Granny passed away, he couldn't bear living without her. He'd rooted himself in the ground by her grave and used magic to raise up the earth. He hadn't stopped using magic until *all* of him had turned into a tree.

"—*not right!*" A harsh voice rose, coming from the front door. It was Sybaline's momma. Tension spiraled through Sybaline, until all at once, she tapped into the magic surrounding her, letting the warmth of it flow into her bones and into her skin. At her summoning, the crisp leaves of fall pasted to her skin and camouflaged her from anyone's notice just like Nettle had done. She crept forward until she met with Nettle, who sat right beside the stairs.

"But that's so soon," Sybaline's momma was saying.

"You've had plenty of warning," said the TVA man.

"Plenty of warning?" said Aunt Ethel, her voice stern enough to make Sybaline cringe into herself. This man clearly didn't know that Aunt Ethel wasn't someone you wanted to make mad. "It's never been real. You know it too! For fifteen years, you've talked about a dam. *Fifteen years!* A *small* dam. You sure built a dam all right, but not a small one. A huge one. A massive one! And it's going to destroy our homes."

"You knew years ago that the plans for the dam changed," he said. "We came and told you how big it would be, and you knew, too, that you would have to leave."

"It's not *leaving*!" Aunt Ethel shouted, making both Sybaline and Nettle jump. The leaves rustled against their skin. "It's abandoning everything that makes us *us*. It's being forced to give up the past century of work we've done here."

Sybaline knew what Aunt Ethel was saying: If they left the valley, they'd give up their magic. This was the only place any of them knew this sort of magic existed.

"I'm sorry for that," he said. "I really am—"

"You aren't," Momma said. "If you were, you wouldn't be doing this."

The TVA man sighed. He sounded tired, as if he'd been accused of not being sorry before. "Compensation for your land is in the bank and will stay there until you take it out."

Aunt Ethel said, "I've seen what waits for me in the bank, and it's not nearly enough to equal the two hundred acres of land you're taking from me."

Momma said, "And our family graves haven't been moved like you promised. You said the cemetery would be relocated, so our ancestors wouldn't end up underwater."

"Our workers have been busy. They've had hundreds of graves to relocate, but they should be by soon to move yours."

The man took a step back, glancing between all of the women. "Look. The dam will be completed within the month. If you all aren't gone by then… Well, the valley will flood either way."

Sybaline's momma and aunts stayed quiet at that.

"I'm really am sorry for it." His shoulders drooped, as if pushed down by heavy hands. "I truly am. If there were a way for you to keep your land, we would've figured it out, but there isn't. Once the dam is running, electricity will go directly to the aluminum plants. It'll help the war effort, and we need all the help we can get. Some of your husbands are away at war. You can't argue against helping them the best we can. The world will be a safer place because of this dam."

Sybaline thought of Poppa, of the fighting he was doing that she didn't quite understand. She thought, too, of the fact that once the government flooded her valley to make electricity, her home and the magic would be drowned beneath miles and miles of water.

It didn't make sense. How could destroying the one thing that made her who she was help the war effort? How could ridding the world of this valley make the war easier for Poppa? It certainly didn't make sense how uprooting her from where she belonged would make the world a safer place.

Nettle gripped her arm, stopping the leaves around Sybaline from trembling. Sybaline gripped her hands into tight fists, trying to focus and push away all the terrible thoughts that swirled in her head.

The man said his goodbyes to Momma and the aunts and stepped off the porch, except when he did, he landed straight on top of Sybaline. She yelped, and her concentration broke altogether. The man tried to catch himself against one of the beams along the porch, but he wasn't quite fast enough. Together, he and Sybaline ended up in a pile among the discarded leaves she'd magicked to her skin.

CHAPTER 3

Sybaline's thigh and side ached from where the man had stomped on her, but that didn't hurt near so much as the speed with which her heart raced. It pounded against her ribs, a tiny squirrel trying to claw its way free of a cage. Nettle popped out of her own leaf pile and grabbed Sybaline by the arms to haul her up.

The TVA man scrambled to his feet, scooping up his floppy hat from where it'd fallen on the ground, and shouted, "*What* are you doing?"

Sybaline cringed, but beside her, Nettle stood tall with her shoulders thrown back. "She didn't mean to be underfoot. We were trying to hear what was happening to our home, considering you're trying to steal it away."

"*Steal?* It's not called stealing, and I'm not the one doing it to you! I'm not the whole government, little girl. I'm only one person, and I'm stuck in the bad spot of giving you this news. What's happening is called eminent domain. The government has the full right to take and use your land." He scrunched his floppy hat in one hand. "We told you years ago this moment was coming. People have already left the valley. Entire families have gone and set roots down elsewhere. You're some of the last people to go."

"It feels an awful lot like stealing," Nettle said.

The man pulled his hat over his brow and smoothed out the brim. After taking a deep, calming breath, he patted Sybaline on the top of the head, almost as if to say that he forgave her for him falling over her. "Think, after you move out of this backwoods place, you'll have so many more opportunities. You'll be able to attend a big school in the city and make lots of new friends. Friends who aren't your cousins! You'll have electricity in your house. You'll even be able to buy shoes. You should be grateful."

Sybaline dug her toes into the grass to hide away her bare feet. She hadn't realized she should feel embarrassed for not liking to wear shoes until right that moment. She didn't much enjoy how it felt.

He nodded to Sybaline's momma and the aunts. "Remember, you have one month. If we have to send the sheriff to evict you, we will." And with that, he turned and disappeared in a direction that would take him to the next family whose lives he had to ruin.

Sybaline's aunts erupted into chaos. Voices clamored over

one another, until Auntie Wooline rose hers above the rest to say, "Much as I hate to admit it, we don't have a choice."

"We always have a choice," said Aunt Ethel.

"We only have *two* choices. Either we walk out of this valley or we swim out, and I'm not so good at swimming as that."

"There's a third choice," Aunt Ethel said, her mouth pressed into a thin line. "We can use our magic and stay."

"And go full-magic? What, you want to transform completely and live beneath the lake as a weed or a plant? No, thank you. I'm not Papaw, and I'm not going to use my magic to become a tree. I like living too much for that."

"I'm saying it's a choice, not that it's a *good* choice."

Sybaline wasn't as sure as Auntie Wooline though. Maybe Aunt Ethel was right—maybe staying in the valley was worth anything, even the threat of transforming.

Beside her, Nettle looped her arm through Sybaline's, and they started to back away slowly. With the aunts arguing, it was possible they could sneak off before they got in trouble for having snooped in the first place.

Of course, Nettle's momma didn't miss anything. Before they could take a second step, she was off the front porch and grabbing Nettle's ear.

"Ow, ow, Momma!" Nettle said, batting at Aunt Wooline's hand.

"Did you think we wouldn't know you were nearby, using magic?" Auntie Wooline said.

"Syb and I wanted to know what was happening," Nettle complained.

"Eavesdropping isn't the right way to find out what's happening. It isn't honest," Sybaline's momma said, nearly too quiet for Sybaline to hear. Except with those hushed words, everyone stopped talking and arguing. Silence descended. Momma took a breath and added, "We've waited as long as we can. It's time to move."

All the feeling in Sybaline's body plummeted straight out of her. She turned numb, including her fingertips where the magic usually hummed warm and friendly. Is this what it would be like not to have magic? Would she be left empty and cold?

She found herself sitting on the edge of the porch, fuzz in her ears keeping out all the words her family said. None of it mattered anyway. What mattered had already happened— Momma had decided they were officially leaving.

Nettle tugged once on Sybaline's braid before she left. She trailed then after her own momma while saying, "Marlys and Tevi ran and hid. No, they're not up a tree, Momma. Well, I mean, they could be up a tree, but they probably went back to the creek. I don't wanna go find them! Why do I have to go get them?"

At last, Sybaline's house was blessedly empty. No aunts

stood on the porch. No TVA man haunted their steps. Only Sybaline and Momma remained.

Footsteps clipped behind her, until Momma stood with her legs at Sybaline's spine. Sybaline leaned back, letting Momma hold up her weight.

"I don't see what's so wrong with my cousins being my friends," Sybaline said. "I don't know why that man said that."

"Nothing's wrong with it. It's just not how everyone lives. Some people live very far away from their family."

"Like Cedric and Benjamin?" Sybaline asked, talking of her two older brothers, one who lived in the city and the other who lived and worked at the dam site.

"Yes, like them. Your brothers are grown, and they made the best choices they could given the circumstances." Momma ran her fingers through the hair on Sybaline's head that refused to stay in her braid. "It's time, Sybaline. We knew this day would come."

"No!" She stood fast enough to make herself light-headed. Everyone else might have known moving day would come, but she never had.

Momma reached out and took hold of Sybaline's shoulders, pulling her into a hug that she resisted at first. After a moment, she tucked herself into Momma's strong body.

Sybaline trembled, unable to stop her muscles from

revealing her nervousness. Instead of telling Momma how awful she felt, she asked, "What's eminent domain?"

"It means the government can take people's land whenever they'd like, all because they're the government."

"That doesn't seem very fair."

"We're not the first people they've done this to, nor will we be the last." Momma put Sybaline away from her, straightening the twisted collar of her dress. "Now, if I'm not mistaken, you have chores to finish before we head to Wooline's for the fish fry tonight. Be the responsible girl I know you to be. Go get the graveyard cleaned up and be respectful about it."

Sybaline locked her teeth together. Questions boiled inside her, but the day was dwindling, and Momma needed her to get her chores done. Instead of saying anything else, she swallowed down her wonderings, gathered up the folds of her dress, and headed down the steps and into the field. Without the TVA man there to stare at her bare feet, she didn't much care that they were darkened with dirt. She didn't need any shoes, not with thick calluses along the bottom of her feet, and no one could convince her otherwise.

With anger at the whole of the situation simmering inside her, she broke into a sprint. She flew, faster and faster with the ground spinning beneath her, turning into a blur that almost made her sick. It felt nearly like the anger in her chest.

Through the woods she went, until she came to the bottom of a steep incline. Panting, she leaned into the hill and made her way up, using trees to drag her body toward the top, some two hundred fifty feet above where she'd started. Once there, she let loose all the pent-up air she'd stored in herself in a giant whoosh, trying to shove out the last of the terrible feelings that had taken root. She never liked to visit the graveyard when she carried anger inside her. It seemed a rude way to say *hello* and *how are you* to her family.

"I'm sorry, Granny," she said at last, her feet not wanting to move toward her granny's grave. "I don't know how to get rid of all the bad feelings. I'm angry, is all. So, so angry."

The top of the hill was small and flat, with trees ringing the edges and providing shade for the graves that made their home on the hillock. Small weeds and shoots surrounded the graves—Granny's and Granny Great's and Aunt Edna's and Uncle Charlie's and her baby sister's who'd died two days after her birth. She looked to Granny's gravestone, which simply read: ALMINY LARK.

Sybaline wiggled her toes into the grass and imagined what Granny might say were she there. In her mind, it went something like, *Hush and stop your worrying. I'm not happy about the situation either, but we'll be okay.*

Crossing over to Granny's grave, she knelt and held out her

hands, the magic returning and foaming inside her. It cleansed away what remained of her mad. She started picking weeds then, allowing the magic to burrow deep to force out all the roots, and while she did, she told her ancestors all the news and gossip. She finished by telling them that their graves would be moved soon.

Moved?

Sybaline's hands froze over the last of the weeds. Her head popped up, and she looked at the tree that stood guard behind Granny's grave.

"Papaw Lark?" she asked.

The tree had a slightly Papaw-like shape to it, with his strong back and wide shoulders and knobby nose that had been broken twice, once by his brothers while playing in the woods and once by the lumber yard he'd worked at.

Papaw had raised up the land of the graveyard while turning himself into that tree, but at the time, he hadn't known the valley would be flooded to make electricity through a dam, and he certainly hadn't known the graves would be moved. It would be terrible for Granny to be picked up and taken to some random graveyard in the city and have him be left behind to drown beneath the lake all on his lonesome.

Sybaline choked on her sadness. She pressed her knuckles to her teeth and tried to breathe slow. "I'm sorry," she said to Papaw.

She knew, without having to think on it hard, that the government workers would never move the Papaw-tree along with the graves. They would never understand.

Her body went limp, bones holding her up only because that was their job, and they took it quite serious. This place, this *valley*, was her home. It was her family and her life and all she knew. She felt like Papaw, with magic rising into her body straight from the earth, tying her to the dirt and the water and the green things of the world. It flowed throughout her, into her marrow, then back into the land.

It wasn't that she possessed the mountains, but that she was woven into them and them into her. She was rooted here, and she knew, without even the smallest tremble of doubt inside her, that she couldn't ever, *ever* leave.

CHAPTER 4

Sybaline lied to her momma for the very first time in the morning. It was a small one, but still, it made tangled, noxious plants grow in her chest.

From the angle at which Sybaline stood, she could count the wrinkles in her mother's skin. The puckers of tired beneath her eyes. The torn seam in her collar; Sybaline had never seen a tear in Momma's collar before.

"Nettle asked if I could help pack up their house, since we're already done packing," she said.

Of course, Nettle hadn't asked for help packing. What Sybaline needed was someone to walk to the dam construction site with her. She didn't want to go alone.

Momma nodded, giving Sybaline permission to leave. Momma'd packed up their entire house months before, making them live awkwardly out of open trunks in the living room. She'd hated it—the way her momma was prepared to leave, even though none of them wanted to.

When she arrived at Nettle's family's gristmill, she only meant to ask for Nettle to come with her, but of course, her younger cousins insisted on tagging along as well.

She and Nettle walked through the woods with Marlys and Tevi in tow. The girls were a jangled mess, as alive and noisy as the forest surrounding them. For every yell out of their mouths and every tromp of their feet, the mountains gave one back. Rustling leaves. Chirping birds. Whooshing wind. Golden sunlight that stretched and bent between the treetops to press against their skin. Magic pooled in their palms and tugged grass and flowers in their direction.

Sybaline held it in her hands, warm and comforting against her skin. *This* is what she would fight for.

"I don't know why you said this'll be easy," Nettle said as she walked beside Sybaline, swinging her arms at the same time as Sybaline's, so they matched.

"It won't be hard. We'll find Benjamin and get him to tell us how to stop the dam," Sybaline said. Her older brother had worked on the dam for eighteen months now. He hadn't come home in ages, not even for Christmas. "For all I know, he's been trying to figure out how to stop the construction this whole time."

They came upon a dirt road that led into the one-lane town in the middle of the valley. That town kept enough supplies that it meant Sybaline's family rarely had to make a trip into the city.

Heading in the opposite direction, they walked toward the dam site. The road climbed up the mountainside, switching back on itself as it headed higher toward the sky. After a while, the road stopped inching up the mountainside and cut directly west. Their footsteps fell heavy on the packed dirt, all four of them slowing, though they didn't do so consciously.

Nothing specific marked this place. Nothing told them the valley and the magic ended here. But still, together, they stalled.

It was Nettle who finally drew in a deep breath and took a giant step forward. Then went Marlys, then Tevi, and finally, Sybaline.

The warmth in her palms fell away. Her hands clenched, trying to hold tight to the magic, to bury it deep in her bones, to swallow it whole, but despite the strength of her grip, it slid away. Panic rose steady in her lungs, and she breathed hard through her nose. Shadows landed on her shoulders and chilled her skin, snaking over the warm places the magic had lived.

Breathe through it, Momma said in her mind, in the whispering of wind as it tousled the ends of her hair. *I know it's uncomfortable but breathe through it. Your body will get used to not having the magic.* She'd taught Sybaline how to do this when she was young, to make sure Sybaline understood what was happening when she left the valley, to understand that *You are not losing a part of yourself; it only feels like it.*

Sybaline hadn't left the valley in a very long time—she never had reason to—and she'd forgotten the way the vanishing magic left sad holes beneath her skin. She exhaled hard and took another step. The magic would wait for her. It was her job to move forward, to find a way to protect the valley.

Nettle took Tevi's hand and Sybaline took Marlys's hand and, like this, the four walked down the road and toward a bend that was cleared of trees and brush. A rumble of sound reached them. Machinery roared and crunched and whirred down below over the side of the mountain, puffing plumes of smoke into the air. The mountains were notorious for holding on to that smoke, grabbing it at their tippy-tops and refusing to allow it into the sky. There, it hovered, black and grimy. Unnatural clouds that covered the trees and weren't anything like the white cotton balls that usually hung there. It darkened the insides of Sybaline, turning her heart into an upset, angry mess.

She dragged her gaze from the sickly sky to where the river once ran free. Here, the valley tapered, the mountains closing together, and here, the dam had been constructed.

Men walked all over a massive wall of concrete. Cars drove across its top and cranes sat near its bottom. On the side of the dam on which they stood—the valley's side—the river once flowed. Now, it butted against the back side of the dam and had begun to form a pool that would soon turn into a lake.

Beneath this lake's waters, her home would disappear.

"The dam didn't used to look like this," Marlys said.

"It used to have lots of holes," Tevi said.

"It didn't used to almost be done," Nettle said, "and now, it's almost done."

"I don't like it." Tevi started to cry.

"You don't like a lot of things," Nettle said, though her voice didn't tease like normal.

"Dams should only exist if they're made by beavers," Marlys said.

Sybaline forced her lungs to work, sucking in as deep a breath as she could, the air tasting of grime and steel and a specific tang that made her think of the earth's blood, as if the dam itself were the black suture lines covering over a deep wound.

"We need to find Benjamin," Sybaline murmured on her exhale. She placed the dam at her back and continued along the road, her resolve strengthening even while her body ached even worse for the magic's absence.

The road cut along the mountain above the dam and would soon spit them out at a bustling, makeshift town. Now, all four girls held hands so they strung together in a line. Pulsing her hands three times, Sybaline said a silent *I love you* to the cousins beside her.

Against the welcome sign to the town rested a large poster slathered in black paint that read: WORK OR FIGHT.

"Benjamin works and my poppa fights," Sybaline said. "Neither of them had a choice in the matter. Next, they'll probably take Cedric for some reason or other."

"I heard they take clergymen overseas to pray with the fighting men," Nettle said. "Cedric could go to war and try to pray everybody's way to safety."

Sybaline glared at Nettle, who shrugged and didn't bother apologizing. They both knew it was all too real a possibility that Sybaline's eldest brother could be sent to war.

They continued on, bunching together and stepping off the road when a truck rattled by, kicking dust onto their dresses and into their faces. Coughing, they followed a rise in the road and then paused, looking down on the town.

Hundreds of people, more people than Sybaline had ever seen before, even in the middle of their own town, milled about. It was mostly men, looking as if they were either coming from or going to a hard day's work. There were women too. They wore long, clean dresses, looking as if they hadn't spent their mornings in a garden like Sybaline's momma, but instead were ready to head to church, even though it wasn't Sunday. Children ran about behind them, and Sybaline remembered that some of the men had traveled to the worksite with their families.

"How do we find Benjamin?" Marlys asked, looking over all the people. They'd never walked this far into the makeshift town before. Benjamin had always met them at the place the magic stopped.

"The only way is through." Nettle held tighter to Sybaline's hand and dragged them down the small hill before them.

Nervousness slicked Sybaline's palms and made her hold tighter to Nettle and Marlys. They found themselves in the middle of an intersection, with roads branching in five directions. They took a path that looked less busy than the others and came to a line of white houses.

"They look like cows," Tevi said.

"There aren't any cows here," Marlys said.

Tevi pointed at the house. "It looks like that cow that died in the winter last year and the bones went all white in the sun."

Sybaline laughed, and to her surprise, tension released in her shoulders. For some reason, imagining these houses as the carcasses of cows delighted her. "Who would paint their house the color of bone?"

"Better yet, why paint a house at all?" Nettle asked. "Wood looks nice the color of wood."

All four stood staring at the houses, the bodies of cows standing in a row, abandoned of their meat and left for vultures to pick at, when a sharp voice from behind them said, "Who are you and why are you standing in front of my house?"

CHAPTER 5

Surprised, Sybaline grabbed for the magic, her hands and mind grasping not around the tingling warmth, but around emptiness. It left her stumbling.

A girl with smooth white skin stood behind them, along with a group of kids that looked exactly like one another. Sybaline could hardly tell them apart.

The girl said, "I didn't know they were bringing more workers in, considering the dam's almost done. Who's your family and when'd you move here?"

"We didn't move here," Sybaline said. "We're from the valley, and we're looking for my brother. His name is Benjamin."

"Benjamin Farris?" The girl frowned. "He's ancient, at least forty. He can't be your brother."

"Benjamin *Shaw*. He pours concrete."

"A construction worker? These houses are where important workers live. The engineers and architects. All the construction workers stay in their own area." Her finger drew a line from her house and pointed down the road.

Sybaline hid her hands behind her skirts, folding them into the cloth and hiding the claws her fingers made.

"You're mountain kids, right?" the girl asked.

"I live in the mountains," Sybaline said. It was one thing to call oneself a mountain person, but another thing entirely if someone else said it. She was proud of where she came from and who she was because of it; she had a feeling this girl didn't see it as such, like the TVA man and his *you'll even be able to buy shoes* comment.

"You're mountain kids, and we're dam kids." The girl grinned.

"It's nice living here," said a boy about Tevi's age. "We get to play tennis and go to school, though I still haven't seen a bear. Everyone says there are bears here. Have you seen a bear? Do they look like teddy bears? I think I'd like to have a real bear better than having my teddy bear."

Of course Sybaline had seen a bear before, and of course they didn't look like teddy bears, and oh no *no* this boy would *not* like to have a real bear better than a teddy bear.

"He's right," said another boy. He was older than some of the others, maybe the same age as Sybaline and Nettle. He looked the same way Benjamin had right before he'd grown a foot one summer, all gangly with pointed elbows and knees. His speech was wrong, too, round vowels sneaking into his words in strange places and clipped consonants tightening the sound of the letters. "This is the best place I've ever lived, and I've lived lots of places. Tennessee and North Carolina and even way over in Colorado."

Sybaline knew here was best on earth. She didn't need someone else to say it though.

"It's great," said the girl, "except that my daddy said he watched a man get crushed by a crane a week ago. I could do without stories like that."

The air around Sybaline turned cold and still. That man who had been crushed was one of Cedric and Benjamin's friends. His family hadn't been able to hold the funeral yet, on account of the fact that his body still hadn't been returned to them.

The boy with the odd accent patted the girl on the shoulder, his smile small and timid. "Besides that part, being a dam kid is great. We get to play in the mountains."

"The mountains aren't here for you to *play* in." Sybaline's breath rattled in her chest. "They're not a toy."

The boy's smile slipped away. "I'm proud I'm a dam kid. I think the dam is beautiful, and it'll help win the war."

"How could a dam win a war that's happening ten thousand

miles away?" She didn't give the boy time to answer, because she'd heard the answer many times before. "It's ugly and terrible, and it's set on destroying my life."

The girl stepped forward, moving close enough to make Sybaline uncomfortable. "What do you know about it? You're just a mountain kid. You don't know anything about the world."

Sybaline opened her mouth, but instead, Nettle grabbed her hand and pulled. Sybaline allowed herself to be dragged away from the awful kids.

"I've never heard you talk so sharp before, much less to perfect strangers," Nettle said.

"I don't know what you mean." Sybaline struggled to contain the rush of emotions that spun through her.

"*The mountains aren't here for you to play in,*" Nettle said, mimicking her.

"That's true though!" Tevi said. "Remember when Bernie kept playing in the trees and Auntie Pauline kept saying, 'Don't you play in the trees, Bernie. You're gonna fall outta one someday and break your arm,' but Bernie kept playing and sure enough, she fell and broke her arm. Remember?"

They all remembered. Cousin Bernie had been insufferable the entire time her arm healed. As much as they'd grown up having fun in the mountains, they all knew that in the end, the mountains weren't a toy to fool with.

They walked in silence, pushing through the crowd, and heading in the direction the girl had pointed.

"Someone's following us," Tevi said suddenly, talking around a mouthful of bread she'd pulled from her pocket. Sybaline wondered what other snacks she had stashed in there.

Sybaline turned, searching for who might be following them, and from the crowd of people churning about the street, the boy with the strange accent appeared. It was the play-in-the-mountains boy, as if he *knew* the valley. People thinking the mountains were theirs were what turned the mountains into a wasteland. Sybaline's family had watched it happen before, like when lumber companies had come in and ripped up all the trees, turning every inch of the valley into a barren field.

Sybaline's shoulders rose toward her ears as she waited for the boy to reach them. When he did, he stood, all strange eyes and bony limbs and pale cheeks that looked like they'd never been burned by the sun. He held out one hand, stiff and formal. "I'm Herbert Fisch. My friends all call me Fisch though. You can too."

"I'm Sybaline Shaw." Sybaline peeled her hand away from where it'd glued tight to her side and forced it open, pressing her palm to his, wanting the warmth of the magic against her skin rather than his dry fingers.

"I'm Nettle." Nettle shook his hand, too, pumping it up

and down in a way that looked uncomfortable for Fisch and hilarious for Nettle.

"I can give you a tour!" Fisch said, a bit breathless, as if he'd been holding back the words and they'd rushed out without his permission. "I know you don't like the dam, but I thought if you saw it, you might understand how important it is."

"You sound like the pamphlets the government mailed," Sybaline said.

"All I want is to help," he said, fidgeting.

Sybaline looked at Nettle, eyebrows raised, silently asking, *What do you think?*

And Nettle looked back blank, saying, *Dunno. You figure it out.*

Sybaline stopped herself from growling in frustration. She'd intended on finding Benjamin first, but this boy could provide her with information about the dam, and she wasn't about to miss the opportunity. She said, "I would very much appreciate a tour of the dam."

Fisch broke out in a smile that crinkled his eyes. "I know everything about it! I'll be your tour guide."

Sybaline stopped herself from sarcastically saying *Oh, goody.* Sometimes when she was mad, it made nice-sounding words come out of her mouth with a cruel-sounding bent, and she had a feeling this boy wouldn't know how to understand it.

Fisch stuffed his hands into his pockets. His clothes were crisp, pressed into flat lines free from wrinkles and dust, and Sybaline wondered if he'd ever gotten dirty in his life. He headed down the road. "Before, we were out of class for lunch," he said, "I'm happy to skip for a bit, even though if I do, Kitty'll probably tattle on me."

"You're skipping school?" Nettle asked with a grin. "Wise choice."

The boy echoed her smile. "My dad says that sometimes, a person needs a break from work."

"My dad says that high work ethic shows the worth of a person," Sybaline said, nice-sounding words that really weren't nice at all slipping free without her control.

Nettle elbowed her in the side, hard. Sybaline clutched her ribs, but she didn't regret talking. Her dad did used to say that phrase a lot, especially when he mentioned his family that lived over in the city.

Herbert Fisch wore an uncertain sort of smile now, quirking higher on one side of his mouth than the other. Waving down a road that led toward the place where the workers lived, he said, "They built this village for the workers from scratch. Did you know they had to build *roads* through the valley to get here? Of all the places my dad has moved us to, this is by far the most remote. Dad was one of the first to move in, because of how good he is at planning dams. This is the sixteenth one he's helped build!"

It was like Fisch was bragging but didn't quite know it, and he was bragging about something he had absolutely no hand in. If his dad was good at building dams, it certainly wasn't because Herbert Fisch existed.

"They'd been planning on making a dam here for decades to help control flooding," Fisch said. "But when the war started up, it kicked everything into motion. The dam will create a ton of electricity, and all that electricity will be sent to the aluminum plants, and the aluminum plants will make ships and planes and—"

"We already know this."

"I like talking about it, is all," he said, his pale cheeks flushing, heat bleeding into his ears.

They trailed after Fisch, stepping off into the grass when workers clogged the road. They headed down the mountainside until at last they took a small turn and there, a slate-gray wall rose before them. It branched between the mountains, connecting the two sides of the valley Sybaline lived in, and a massive road sat atop the cement.

Sybaline's feet slowed. In the mountains, she felt tiny but also part of the wider world. Before this wall, she felt tiny and also meaningless.

Fisch walked backward so he faced them and said, "Now that the dam's complete, people can walk on the top. They made it wide enough that two big military vehicles can drive side by side on it." With a big, dramatic step, he headed onto the wall. "It's a half mile long and four hundred eighty feet tall. When the lake is filled up, it'll be about one hundred and thirty feet deep, but there might be places that are as deep as *four hundred* feet! That sounds huge, doesn't it? Sometimes, though, numbers don't give a very clear picture of how big something is." Fisch stretched his arms out wide, as if he were trying to encompass the entire dam. "Half a mile sounds short, but when you look straight out, it looks long. Four hundred eighty feet sounds deep, but when you look over the edge, it looks even deeper."

At the far end of the dam, the workers looked like minuscule ants. Sybaline went to the side and peered over the edge at the place where the river was supposed to flow out.

"It took five thousand people to build this," Fisch said. "They completed it in thirty-six months, working constant, no breaks, not even during the night or on holidays."

Sybaline walked to the other side, counting each of the long steps it took to get there. She looked down, down, down at the valley—*her* valley—far below. There, water gathered, dark and angry against the bottom of the dam, as if it were knocking against the cement, asking to get out.

How was she supposed to destroy this monstrous thing and save her valley? She didn't think coming here would make her feel so very powerless. In a rush of anger, she kicked the cement guardrail of the dam, then punched it, too, for good measure, letting the physical pain of it smash against the pain inside her.

"I don't think that's going to work," Nettle said.

Sybaline sucked on her knuckles, which hurt doubly more than her toes did. She wanted to scream at the dam. Scream and scream until the cement cracked straight through. Whipping around to face Fisch, who had the audacity to look aghast at her burst of anger, she said, "I want this thing taken down. If you know so much about this dam, tell me how to make it go away."

"Even if I knew, I'd never tell you," he said. "It's important, and it's not coming down."

"My home is the most important thing to me, and it's going to be underwater soon."

"My dad's job is the most important thing to me, and he builds dams."

"Your dad's *job* is most important to you?"

"You're the one who values some plot of land over everything else. Even over winning the war!"

"Don't you *dare* say that. My poppa's fighting in that war."

"Which means you should care about winning it."

45

"I care about winning plenty, but I care about my home too!"

"It's not like this valley is the only valley to be flooded," he said. "There are dozens of others already gone, and there will be more that disappear too. More dams are going to be made."

"Is it supposed to make me feel better knowing that dozens of valleys and thousands of people's homes are gone?"

"You're acting like you're the only person to lose your house."

"My *home*, not just my house. It's my home. It's the valley and the trees and the sun and the way snow freezes on one side of the valley but melts on the other during winter—"

"You can find that somewhere else. Go live in another valley. There's nothing special about yours."

Sybaline spoke through clenched teeth, "And your daddy is nothing special either. He moves around all the time. He's never even given you a *real* home."

Fisch's face filled with intense hurt, and before Sybaline quite knew what was happening, he turned and fled away from them, running straight across the dam.

"Hear me out," said Nettle, watching as Herbert Fisch ran and ran, not slowing once the entire half mile it took to reach the opposite side. "As much as he might've deserved that, considering how rude he'd been, you maybe took things a bit too far."

CHAPTER 6

"It's not my fault he got his feelings hurt," Sybaline said, knowing exactly how dumb the words were as they came out of her mouth.

"You should've done a good belly breath before you said mean words." Tevi patted her tummy and breathed through her nose. "That's what I do when I'm mad."

Tevi was right; Sybaline should've paused before speaking. She pressed the heel of her hand against her forehead, trying to push deep all the fruitless anger that had filled her at seeing the dam. That anger had taken hold of her tongue, and she didn't like what it'd made her say to Fisch.

Now that she'd taken a few clear breaths, she found she understood something important about Herbert Fisch: He had no idea what sort of life she lived. He was stuck in his world of dams and construction, and no part of him bothered to understand there was another side to the story that was being told.

His story was not the only story that mattered.

Sybaline's home was made up of stories. Of her family moving to the United States. Of finding the valley and learning to work magic. Of Papaw loving Granny Alminy. Of Poppa meeting Momma and seeing her bring the valley to life for the first time. Of the family gathering and working magic to encourage life back into the valley and make it whole again after the logging companies tore through. All their stories wove together, making an entire history that was as tied into the earth as Sybaline was herself.

Fisch didn't know any of that, and Sybaline had yelled at him because of it.

"*Sybaline!*" a voice shouted from somewhere behind her.

Surprised, Sybaline twisted around, turning her head fast enough to make her dizzy.

"Sybaline!" Benjamin yelled again, and this time, Sybaline spotted the hands he waved in the air.

Relief poured through her, shaking her arms and fingers, which she quickly clenched. She ran down the road back the way they'd come, her gaze locked tight on her brother. Grime covered his skin and sweat dampened his shirt. She launched into his arms, and he squeezed her tight.

Sybaline loved both her big brothers, but Benjamin had loved their home as much as she did, while Cedric had always been eager to leave the valley. Had Benjamin been home, Sybaline wouldn't have been quite so alone in her fight to rescue the magic.

"You're taller," she said, muffled against his shoulder where she pressed her face.

"Why are you here?" His voice buzzed through his chest, vibrating against her cheek. "What was Momma thinking, letting you walk here? This is a work camp!"

Sybaline drew into herself as he set her down. Why was he not glad to see her? "I walk all over the mountains and valley by myself. I'm perfectly fine."

"You're not perfectly fine. You don't understand how dangerous it can be here. There was a riot just last week."

"Why?"

Benjamin shifted, looking uncomfortable. "Management is bringing in Black construction workers, and some of the white men here are mad over it."

"Not you though?"

"No, Syb. I stay far away from the men who get mad over that sort of thing. Everyone deserves to have a good job and to be safe at their place of employment." He crouched down a little so they stood eye to eye. He didn't look quite as he did in her memory. His face was a little less soft, and his shoulders were a little more broad and his eyes were a little

49

more creased at the edges, just in the same way Poppa's and Momma's were.

"Is it dangerous for you here?"

"No, but…" He stood and ran a hand through his hair, leaving all the crusty pieces sticking up.

From behind Sybaline, Tevi laughed and said, "You look like a scarecrow."

Benjamin's face paled. "You brought *Tevi*?"

"Nettle and Marlys too," Sybaline said.

"Bless it, Sybaline. You're trying to kill me. This isn't a place for children."

"We met a bunch of kids up the hill—"

"Sybaline! Those kids don't count. They aren't like *you*."

"What's wrong with *me*?"

Benjamin stared at her.

"What's wrong with me?" she asked, quieter now.

"I don't mean something's wrong with you, Syb. People know those kids here. No one knows you."

The world pressed against Sybaline's shoulders, heavy and suffocating and confusing.

"Sybaline Shaw, spit out what you came here for while I walk you down the road. I just got off shift and am hungry, and now I'm worried about you."

Reluctantly, she turned to walk beside him, her shoulder only coming up past his elbow. "The government man came by yesterday and told us the dam would be finished in a month. Momma said we're moving now." They only had *one month* to save their home.

Benjamin slowed, his head dropping so his chin rested against his chest. Then he turned toward her. "I work on the dam. Don't you think I know it's almost finished?"

Sybaline's gaze shifted away from Benjamin's face. She knew he worked on the dam, but that didn't mean he *wanted* to work on it. He hadn't been drafted to fight in the war, and he'd needed a job, but with the lumber companies all moved out of the valley, *this* was the only job he'd been able to find. He hadn't had a choice. Surely he wanted it gone.

"I'm well aware of the dam's progress. I know it'll be done soon, and I know that means our family is moving."

"If you knew, then why didn't you do something to stop it?" Sybaline's anger spiraled back through her. Why was everyone giving up on their home and the magic so easily? She thought Benjamin would fight beside her.

"What was I supposed to do?"

"Something! *Anything*. You're giving up! You're handing our home over to perfect strangers."

"All I've done is accept there's another way to live that doesn't include dying inside that valley. Helping the war is the most important thing I can do."

51

The war again… Why was the war taking everything from her? She'd meant to come here and get Benjamin's help, and instead, she'd found a version of Benjamin she didn't recognize: He wanted the dam to exist. He wanted their home gone. "After we leave, the dam'll destroy the valley. We'll never be able to go back." She leaned close. "The magic will be gone *forever.*"

Benjamin set one heavy hand on her shoulder, though he released his hold when she twisted away. "Remember the fire, Syb?"

The fire had happened years ago, but not too many years for Sybaline not to have clear memories of it. She well knew the way smoke had clouded over the sun, turning it into a glowing, hazy ball, and the way ash had worked its way into all the folds of their clothes. The fire had raged over the mountains for days. To survive, their family had gathered at Nettle's family's gristmill where water ran through their waterwheel, and Aunt Ethel had held back the flames with her magic. In consequence, a tangle of leafy vines had grown over her shoulders. She rarely used magic now, not wanting to risk the vines growing more and overtaking her body.

"Sometimes what we see as destruction is really a way for the world to create new life," Benjamin said, referring to the way the valley had flourished in the wake of the fire.

"The dam isn't the same thing as the fire," she said. "Humans made the dam!"

"Humans might've made the fire too. Fire and water are both natural parts of the world, and so are wildfires and floods. Wildfire always brings new life, even if it seems like total destruction at first. Who knows what this flood will allow for in the valley? The valley will be fine without us. The world doesn't need us, and the magic sure doesn't either. It's time for us to go and let the valley alone to take care of itself. Our fight's over now."

"I want the dam gone," she hissed. "I want to save the valley. I want to save *us*!"

Benjamin looked at her sideways, exactly the same way her mother did when she wasn't happy with her. "You're trying to save yourself. That's not the same thing, and it's not nearly as noble."

"What do you know about being noble?"

"I know that sometimes it means doing a thing you don't actually want to do."

"I don't like brushing my hair," Tevi said from where she trailed behind them. "But sometimes I do it anyway."

Sybaline's head ached from pressure building behind her eyes, from the clench of her teeth and the tightness of the muscles in her neck. Benjamin had saved her once, way back when he still lived at home. Snow had fallen one winter morning and ice had crusted over the surface of a lake. What an oddly beautiful world it'd been, pure white with clouds blanketing the sky and frost covering the trees and clouds of condensation puffing from her mouth. The curious thrill that had filled her broke as soon as the ice had given way beneath her. She'd been too little to save herself, but Benjamin had been there. He'd always known how to help her, even when she didn't know how to help herself.

When had her brother stopped wanting to help?

The road went by beneath their feet, moving as if on its own accord, until at last, they came upon the place where the magic lived. One more step and they would return to the valley.

Marlys and Tevi rushed forward, screeching and whooping and launching themselves down the road. Nettle did a cartwheel and landed clean on her feet. Sybaline took a big step, and when her foot landed, warmth and comfort tickled in her belly as the magic returned. Joy flooded her skin, almost as if a tiny sun lived in her chest and radiated beams of light from her fingers.

"Benjamin, see? Isn't this place worth savin—" She spun and stopped talking when she saw her brother. "Benjamin?"

He stood stiffly with palms pressed to his thighs. His skin had a sheen to it, beads of sweat breaking out on his brow.

"Are you okay?" Sybaline asked.

"I can't walk into the magic, Sybaline."

"But it's right here." She opened her hands, pulling more

into her palms and brightening the feel of the world. She reached toward him—

"*Stop.*"

With both hands held midair, she froze. Dread inched up her spine. "You...*can't?*"

"I don't want to." Benjamin took a step backward. "I've already adjusted to life without it. I can't go back and force myself to experience that all over again. I'm sorry, Sybaline. I can't walk with you any farther." A crooked smile formed on his mouth, twisting his face. "I'll see you after you've moved. I'll come visit you in the city. I promise."

And with that, her brother waved, turned, and slowly grew smaller as he walked down the road, and Sybaline was left behind, forgotten.

CHAPTER 7

Returning to the valley meant returning to the world's natural rhythm, a heart set to a steady beat, unbroken and unhurried. It thrummed against the soles of Sybaline's feet, pressure that made her aware of her own thready pulse within her.

The waterwheel on Nettle's family's gristmill was working steady as they came upon it, churning beneath the force of the stream that ran beside their house. The wheel itself was a water-powered turbine. It made electricity that was necessary to run the machinery inside the house that ground corn into meal.

She dropped Nettle, Marlys, and Tevi off at home, not bothering to stay, because as soon as they stepped within view of the front door, Auntie Wooline hollered at them for going without telling her. Nettle hollered back, "I left a note! It must've gotten sucked out a window by the wind!"

Sybaline walked upstream, leaving the gristmill and creek behind, crossing through the woods toward her own home. The familiar shape of her log cabin fortified her heart with joy.

"He was here yesterday! He said we had a month!" Momma's voice came from the side of the house where her garden thrived.

The moment of comfort Sybaline'd had at arriving home passed, dread nesting inside her chest.

"I know, Mrs. Shaw," said a man—it was *Sheriff Hart*.

Why was the sheriff at their home? Had he brought news of her daddy?

Sybaline scurried around her house and ducked low to peek around the corner. Sheriff Hart stood beside stalks of corn, his shoulders slumping right along with the heat-tired grain.

"Most people have a month," Sheriff said. "Your property is at the lowest point of the valley though. It'll be the first house to go."

The muscles in Sybaline's legs quivered. Her body weakened, and she sagged against the side of the house.

"They finished the dam a few days ago. The water's already rising," Sheriff said.

"I hear you," Momma said. It sounded a lot like she was forcing calm into her words. "I do. I might be upset about it, but I know it's time to go."

Sheriff exhaled loud. When Sybaline looked, it was to see his face red and eyes damp and posture stooped even worse than the corn. "Thank you. I couldn't stand having to tell Frank that you'd refused to leave."

Sheriff must've been worried Momma was about to decide to stay with the land and drown beneath the water, that he'd have to tell Poppa what Momma had done.

"Are the Rothfords still giving you trouble?" Momma asked.

"They're refusing to leave."

"People make their own choices. You can't force them to choose otherwise."

"I'll have to arrest them and cart them into the city."

Momma smiled, all grinning teeth that looked more angry than happy, reminding Sybaline of the sharp fangs of the dragons Marlys and Tevi liked to draw. "They'll never forgive you."

"Their forgiveness isn't what I'm looking for. I'm trying to save their lives."

"In trying to save their lives, you might kill them."

Sheriff pulled back his shoulders, but even still, his spine stayed curved, the bones too weathered to hold him up straight.

Momma tucked away her grin, covering her teeth with her lips and bending to pick a basket off the ground.

"All right, then," Sheriff said.

"All right, then," Momma said.

"*No,*" Sybaline whispered.

Sheriff said his goodbyes, but Sybaline didn't pay attention. She was focusing too hard on the feel of the earth beneath her. Stone pressed into her palms, lending her strength. Wind whispered against her neck and twirled the ends of her hair. The grass against her knees pricked through her dress and into her skin, saying, *no, no, no*. The magic lived and breathed within her.

She gathered all the magic she could to herself, wrapping it against her in lengths of spun warmth, until Momma said, "You stop that, Sybaline Shaw."

Sybaline let go of the magic and climbed to her feet.

"Cedric is coming tomorrow." Momma pressed her thumb and middle finger to the soft, wrinkled place between her brows. "He's going to borrow a truck from one of his church members, since he usually rides his bicycle in the city. He'll be here early."

Panic laced the inside of Sybaline's chest. Was tomorrow the end of things? Were they moving for good…*tomorrow*? The magic came to her fast when she reached for it, resting against her skin and holding her fear at bay.

"Sybaline. *Stop*. Stop with the magic!"

Even though it made everything in her ache, Sybaline stretched her fingers wide, forcing herself to relinquish her hold on the magic.

"By tomorrow, we need every last thing we own to be packed away," Momma said. "We won't be able to cart everything to town in one trip. The kitchen chairs and table will need a ride of their own, along with the bed frame. My daddy made those, and I won't leave them behind."

"Papaw made the house too," Sybaline said.

Momma peered up at the sloping roof of the house, at the place where a thick beam traveled from one end to the other and at the place where a small star had been carved against the grain. *A light to guide you*, Papaw used to say. *For when the Smokies are smoking, and you can't see the real stars up in the sky.*

"Momma?" Sybaline asked, sure this would be it...the moment Momma would give in and admit they couldn't leave. Together, they would find a way to fight.

"Some things," Momma murmured, "we'll have to figure out how to say goodbye to."

───────

Cedric arrived early the next day, and neither Sybaline nor Momma were ready. They'd packed all night: into a trunk went a dress, a quilt, a tablecloth; away went the handheld corn mill, the set of spoons, the tin plates; down went the heavy iron, the well-worn Bible, the set of needles Momma used to sew up the holes in Sybaline's dresses when she wore the fabric too thin.

The entire time, Sybaline thought of the magic and how it spun inside the dirt and the trees and the wilding blackberry vines and the burgundy sumac, stripped free of leaves in winter. It was inside every piece of the valley, inside *her*.

"I'm tired," Sybaline said, scrubbing at her eyes.

"You look it." Cedric stood in the doorway, one of Papaw's chairs in each hand. He was her eldest brother, three years older than Benjamin. Now he lived in the city, where he was a preacher.

"You should be happy about moving," Cedric said. "The apartment you'll live in will have electricity. You'll like that." He stepped out of the house and headed toward the truck, calling over his shoulder, "You'll love living in the city."

Sybaline stuck her tongue out at Cedric's back, even as she followed him out the door. Nobody else who lived in the valley cared much about the magic. All the people who knew of it tended to take it as something natural, as something that had always existed. It wasn't like it hurt people, and it wasn't like the Larks used it for anything untoward. Cedric had thought magic was a thing that shouldn't exist though. He hadn't liked it, and so he'd gotten out.

"You'll like your new home," Cedric insisted, as he set the chairs in the truck, right beside the table and bed frame, leaving the house all the emptier for it.

"How do you know I'll like it?" Sybaline asked.

"I moved, and I'm happy."

"I'm not *you*."

Cedric turned, shading his eyes from the sun that glared down over the roof of the house. "Have you considered that moving might help you find a better version of you?"

"Why would I need a better version of me?"

"All this magic." Cedric gestured at the mountains. "It can't be good for a person."

"It's good for me."

"You don't know that."

"*I do.*"

Cedric shook his head. His neatly trimmed hair and smooth face didn't match the ruggedness of the mountains. He looked out of place here, and his words made Sybaline feel confused.

She straightened her fingers and drew the earth toward her, tugging at it the slightest so that everything around—the trees with their barely clinging leaves; the kudzu vines with their green, undying leaves; the wildflowers that would bloom straight until first frost—bent toward them.

Cedric didn't notice.

For Sybaline, happiness didn't exist without the magic. She *was* the magic and she *was* the valley, and there wasn't anything in her that would exist without either of them. She wasn't like Cedric, or like Benjamin, or even like Poppa, who'd been able to leave their home like it'd been easy.

She would prove to everyone that their home was worth saving and that she would figure out a way to do it.

Cedric squeezed a few last items into the truck bed, then held out a hand to help Momma into the passenger seat. She stepped up, folding her skirts into her lap and laying her hands flat against her thighs.

"This will be great." Cedric shut the door. "We'll live down the street from each other. Momma, you'll be able to help Gertrude with the kids. She needs to learn how to make your sausage and biscuits. You know how I've missed eating your cooking."

Momma's face shifted, muscles firming along her jaw. "I'm sure Gertrude doesn't need me stepping on her toes. She's perfectly able to raise your children and cook all by herself."

"But your sausage and biscuits. She should learn how to make those."

She glanced out the window at Sybaline—Syb who had learned how to make Momma's sausage and biscuits when she was five and stood beside the kitchen counter on a chair so she could see proper.

Cedric started the truck, and the rumble of the engine caught Sybaline off guard. It sounded like a roar, the same sort of growl she imagined a very upset lion might make.

Sybaline couldn't stomach watching the pieces of their

house rattle against one another in the bed of the truck, but her momma expected her to travel to the city to see their apartment for the first time. Stepping up on the back silver bumper, she slid in awkwardly among the bed frame and kitchen table.

Cedric started driving, and she turned to look at her receding house. No smoke plumed out of the chimney. No light glinted inside the windows. No movement of human shadows worked in the garden.

It was lifeless. Dead. *Drowned.*

The world spun past her. Trees blurred into a shock of color, an autumn rainbow both dull and brilliant at once. Soon enough, they drove down a road that snaked along the wide river the dam was stoppering up. Water lapped at the bank and spilled onto the grass that usually only saw the river's innards when it flooded.

The water's already rising, Sheriff Hart had said. Hearing those words was monstrously different than seeing the water that ran over the banks of the river. It moved faster than Sybaline could track with her eyes.

Fear made her grab for the magic. But then—*snap.* The magic pulled away from her; they entered the world where it no longer existed. She fell into the back of a chair, rungs digging into her ribs. *Breathe through it. Your body will get used to not having the magic; you are not losing a part of yourself; it only feels like it.*

The magic was gone, and Sybaline was less than she'd been a moment before.

She lay against the chair, even though it pressed into her in a painful sort of way. Tears slid down her cheeks and into her mouth. It was silly, really; she'd forgotten the magic would be left behind.

By the time they left the swelling river and followed another, crawled up a mountain, wound along green cow pastures, took countless turns that made Sybaline want to vomit, and passed through the smoky exhalations of the trees, Sybaline's face was dry of tears.

"We're almost into the city," Cedric called out his window. They came to a stop at a T in a road that had more cars driving down it than Sybaline had ever seen before. "Turn around and face forward so you can see the skyline. The buildings make a nice outline against the horizon."

She turned, noticing how the trees had started to thin along the street. The dirt road turned into slick black asphalt that made the truck stop shaking and bouncing quite so bad. Houses popped up along the road, much the same bone-white color as the ones Tevi had called cows in the dam village. Then, between one breath and the next, the city appeared.

"Just as good as the mountains, right, Sybaline?" Cedric called.

Sybaline didn't bother to respond. She was too busy running her gaze along the outline of the buildings before her. This place was only *just as good* as the mountains if a person compared them only in simple words. They both had an outline—treetops against the sky, buildings against the sky. They both had homes—log cabins built as unique as the people inside them, houses identical one to the next. They both had people—people who worked alongside the earth, people who were separate from the earth. But they weren't the same at the heart.

This place looked as if it'd been built elsewhere and plopped onto the land, wiping away trees and squashing flowers in the process. In it, Sybaline could find no magic.

They took a right on the main road that cut through the middle of the busy city and drove down a few streets until they came to a house Sybaline recognized. Cedric had taken his log cabin with him when he'd moved to the city, three years before. Poppa had helped. They'd pulled down each piece of lumber and carted it to his new plot of land, sticking it right beside the church he preached at. Now, the logs were the same shape they'd been years before, except they'd been painted the same shade of white as the church.

"Get on out, Sybaline," Cedric said. "Momma and I are heading to the bank. Gertrude is expecting you inside the house."

Frowning, Sybaline climbed out of the truck, her knees nearly collapsing from having been frozen in a cramped position for so long. She stood beside Momma's window, not wanting to be left behind. Momma's windblown hair formed a disheveled cap on her head, and her whole body seemed to quiver, a slight uncomfortable shivering of her limbs, as if she had a cold brought on by dark winter days.

"Go on in, Sybaline," Momma said, and Cedric took the opportunity to pull off down the road.

CHAPTER 8

Sybaline walked over the threshold of her brother's home and stood in the front foyer, her feet unsure of where they should take her. She glanced at a picture on the wall. Papaw and Granny Alminy and even Granny Great bunched together, along with a host of people Sybaline wasn't quite sure she had names for. Leaning close, she spotted a man with flowers sprouting from beneath the hat he'd plopped onto his head. To anyone who didn't know their family, they might think he was wearing a crown a child might make from wildflowers, but Sybaline knew better—they grew straight from his scalp.

"Magic used in unnatural ways," Gertrude said.

Sybaline jumped, spinning to find the sister-in-law she'd only met a handful of times hovering behind her. She wiped flour-coated hands on a towel.

Sybaline looked back at the picture. Her great-uncle Bo had fallen in love with a girl down in the valley and had grown her springtime flowers in the middle of winter. Frost had dusted the stems and snow had rimmed the petals. They'd glowed crisp sunshine bright with magic filling their thin, flower veins.

She said, "All he did was fall in love."

Gertrude snorted and shook her towel at Sybaline. "Falling in love was *not* what he did, and you well know it. Love was what his heart and body felt, growing flowers and keeping them alive throughout winter was what he did. It wasn't right."

Sybaline turned away from the picture and met Gertrude's stare. "I don't want to move here."

"Of course you don't. You're a Lark, even though you've got your daddy's name. Larks never want to move. Cedric didn't *want* to move, but he sure needed to. He never liked having the magic; it was too much for him. So, he moved, and he's been a happier person for it, exactly as I knew he'd be."

Blazing annoyance built in Sybaline. She headed for the front door, saying, "I'm going to go wait outside for my momma."

"You may not want to move, but you sure need to, just like your brother," Gertrude called after her.

The door slammed behind Sybaline, shutting Gertrude behind it.

Sybaline sprawled beneath a tree, and at some point when the sun sat heavy above her, Cedric returned. "The apartment is beautiful," he said of her new home, adding, "You'll love it. *It will make you happy.*" And for the first time in Sybaline's life, she wanted to punch someone who wasn't Nettle.

She hadn't been sure what an apartment was, but as soon as she saw it, she knew it wasn't meant for her. The building, red bricks stacked two stories high, had small windows lining the front with shades drawn down, eyelids closed and blocking out the sun. She climbed the steps that ran along the outside of the building and walked in the open front door. Momma stood stock-still in the middle of a room that was empty but for their kitchen table and chairs.

"This is it?" Sybaline asked.

Momma frowned. "This is home."

Sybaline recoiled.

"Seventy-two acres of land." Momma leaned against the back of a chair. "We had seventy-two acres of land. A beautiful house. A garden that provided for a family. A mountain rise and a pasture to feed cattle. Seventy-two acres and this is all the government gave us."

"It's fair market price," Cedric said, moving Sybaline out of the doorway.

"I listened just fine when the banker told me it was fair

market price. I don't need you repeating his words." Momma speared Cedric with a glance and folded her arms tight. Wisely, Cedric kept his mouth shut and didn't say anything else. He turned to make his way back down the steps to haul up the rest of the chairs. They had to knock on the doors of the people who lived downstairs to get help carrying up the bed frame and kitchen table. The people hadn't spoken much, had only said enough for Sybaline to gather that they had a daughter about Sybaline's age who she'd soon go to school with.

After they settled each of the things Papaw had built in the apartment, Cedric drove them home, and this time, he didn't bother narrating out the window to Sybaline. This time, Sybaline had the bed of the truck to herself.

This time, she'd seen the sort of life the government wanted her to have, and she knew she wouldn't survive it.

It was as they came to the place where the road formed a T that they passed another vehicle. Sybaline knew it as soon as she heard the rumbling coming toward them, and she sat up in the bed to peer forward. Red and dented, with Nettle's daddy's long hair getting sucked out the driver's-side window and Auntie Wooline's stern face just visible through the dusty front glass, it was the truck that usually stayed at the gristmill. It turned onto the road, revealing a packed bed with Nettle and Marlys and Tevi squeezed in among the trunks.

The trucks passed one another. Nettle's hands stayed still in her lap, not lifting in a wave. Their gazes met. Anger bit through their expressions.

I'm not moving, Sybaline said with her eyes.

Me neither, Nettle seemed to say with hers.

Then they passed and were gone, and Sybaline was returning to the place they *all* belonged.

Sybaline closed her eyes and let the landscape swoop by her, breathing and breathing and breathing until *at last* warmth and movement and life filled her lungs. The magic returned to her, soothing the burning anger in her chest. The tension that had tightened her muscles bled out of her shoulders, but despite how fast the magic's comfort pushed it away, it lingered in the pit of her stomach. She knew that no matter what, if she were to live in that apartment with Momma, she would always feel that—wretched and rigid and missing all the best parts of her. She exhaled until she forced out every drop of air from her chest, then sucked in a clean, magic-filled breath, and when she did, it was filled once more with her determination to save the valley.

It rained that night. A flooding that dragged the sky straight down to the earth. They met with a crash that turned the ground outside Sybaline's home spongy and sodden, much like her clothes on wash day—all drippy and needing to be wrung out.

She watched from the window, asking, "Why did we not ever use our magic to stop the dam?" She thought of Aunt Ethel's words: *There's a third choice. We can use our magic and stay.*

"Attempting that would have turned us all full-magic. There was never a way to stop this from happening; the government is bigger than both us *and* the magic." Momma stoked the fire, keeping the chill inside the empty log house at bay.

"We're not the first they've taken land from, Momma. They shouldn't be able to do that!" Sybaline fisted her hands. "Remember what they did to the Native Americans? You taught me about it, remember? They kicked them off their land and forced them to move and so many of them died."

Momma looked at Sybaline sharp and angry, her glare slicing through the air hard enough to make Sybaline flinch. Her anger was made of the fine, arrow lines of smilax thorns, the vine reaching out to grab and scar if one got too close. "Don't you dare bring up what the government did to the Native Americans like that, Sybaline Shaw. What's happening to us is in no way the same as what happened to them; I know I taught you better than that."

Sybaline dropped her chin, not meeting Momma's eyes.

"For one thing, the government is giving us money for our land—"

"We're hardly getting anything!"

"Would you rather it be nothing? The Native Americans had to walk hundreds of miles away when they were forced out. The government is moving our ancestors' graves, *and* we're keeping our lives. Nobody's killing us or making us walk until we die. You told the TVA man he was stealing our land. They aren't stealing from us, not really, but they sure stole from the Native Americans. What's happening to us is nothing when you take into consideration what's been done to people before."

Sybaline shifted, uncomfortable, and pressed her forehead to the window, streaks of rainwater racing down the glass. Momma was right—she shouldn't have brought up the Native Americans in the way she had. They'd been forced to relocate across the country, and they'd done it on foot. The path they'd taken had been named the Trail of Tears because of how horrible the journey had been.

Momma took up Sybaline's hand and pulled her from the window, sitting them both before the fire.

Sybaline huddled close to Momma's shoulder, taking comfort from her solid body. "It feels like we're giving up, Momma."

"You're mistaking giving up for *surviving*. I've lived a whole lot more life than you, and I've learned that sometimes,

the best thing a person can do is change and adapt. I'm changing and adapting. You best figure out how to do the same,
daughter of mine."

Sybaline shook her head. She knew if she did what Momma
said, it'd mean she was giving up.

"Change isn't always something to fear, Sybaline."

"I'm not scared of change."

"Sometimes a person doesn't know quite what they're
afraid of."

"Do you know what you're afraid of?"

"I always have." Her eyes drifted shut against the flame's
heat. "Your daddy coming home from the war and not knowing
where we've gone."

The ground swooped out from beneath Sybaline. She hadn't
considered it: Was there a chance Poppa wouldn't know where
they'd gone? Surely Poppa would know how to find Cedric, and
Cedric would tell him where they now lived. But still...

Sybaline folded her legs up tight to her chest and watched
as light from the fire passed shadows over Momma's features.
They shifted, quiet and smooth, making her look carved in
wood, roots buried deep in the valley.

Momma said, "Government workers will come in the
morning to unbury our family graves and relocate them to
the city."

Sybaline crunched in on herself, the smallest pieces of her squishing small. Those government workers would come and take away all her ancestors *except* for Papaw Lark. He was stuck where he was, fated to be separated from Granny Alminy forever. He'd drown beneath the water. Sybaline's whole body ached when she thought of it.

"I don't want you there getting in the way or seeing any caskets drawn up from the ground in such a manner. You'll stay home."

"Momma, you shouldn't have to see that either."

"You're not to worry about me." Momma shushed her with a wave of her hand, her face calm and flat as if she felt no emotion, though Sybaline knew that wasn't true. Usually, the calmer Momma got, the more her insides were churned up, just like Sybaline. Except unlike Sybaline, Momma's words didn't slip free and angry, instead they became more controlled. More spare. Quieter and only half saying what she thought.

Sybaline tried to dig beneath Momma's words to find the truth. *You're not to worry about me* could mean any number of things, but to Sybaline, it sounded only as if Momma just didn't want Sybaline there.

CHAPTER 9

Sybaline did her best to sleep light and know when Momma woke, but as always, the night dragged her beneath strange thoughts and the wild magic of the valley. She slept restless amid ferocious dreams. They sparked at the edges and glowed in the middle, and when she woke, the silver taste of spun sugar lingered behind.

She climbed from bed, hurrying after Momma, who'd long since headed to the graveyard. The press of Momma's footprints seemed to be left behind, as if Sybaline could see each step she'd made. Getting dressed. Brushing her hair. Eating over the stove. Making her way out of the house and into the yard, feet smooshing into the soppy grass. As Sybaline followed, she placed her bare feet into the marks Momma left behind. She followed, all her focus bent toward the ground rather than the new, hideous plan that whispered in the silent spaces of her mind.

A truck with large wheels was backed up near the bottom of the graveyard hill. There was no way it could drive up the too-steep incline. They would have to dig up the caskets and lower them down the slope.

Sybaline's belly churned as she found a tree to climb. When she reached the top of the tree, she planted herself against the now-thin trunk and gazed toward the top of the hill. The quiet scene before her was broken only by the lift and fall of the shovels three men swung. The government workers struck the earth, ripping up clods of dirt to spill over the bright green grass. The hill's guts leaked through deep seams, the top of the hill becoming a patchwork of wounds.

Fury tore through Sybaline. How dare they desecrate this place. How dare they dig her family's bones from where they'd found rest. How dare they break the peace and calm that had always lived in the cemetery!

Sybaline lifted her hands, readying the magic at her fingertips, readying herself to push it against the earth and make it impossible for the workers to take her ancestors out of their resting places. If the graves couldn't be moved, surely her aunts would refuse to leave their home. Bending her intent toward shoving the earth back where it belonged, she *pushed* the magic out—

"My latest sun is sinking fast, my race is nearly run." A voice rose into the sky, singing low and sweet. It flowed past Sybaline's ears.

Her breath froze in her chest. She felt the song against her chest.

"My strongest trials now are past, my triumph has begun," coursed Aunt Ethel's strong singing.

Her eyes fluttered shut.

"O come Angel Band, come and around me stand."

She listened hard, finding Auntie Wooline and Auntie Pauline's voice beneath Aunt Ethel's, and last, she found the halting notes of her momma's.

"O come Angel Band, come and around me stand," Momma sang. "O bear me away on your snow-white wings to my immortal home."

There was no anger in Momma's song. No fury. Nothing but sorrow. It turned each note into the same softness that made up butterfly wings, something Sybaline could easily rip and destroy, if she so chose it.

Sybaline's hands fell to her sides. The magic fizzled away, Sybaline only keeping enough of it against her skin to bring her comfort and lessen the ache that spread through her limbs. She cupped her palms against her ears, suddenly needing to block out Momma's voice. Tears dripped down her cheeks. No matter how angry she was, she couldn't hurt her momma.

Turning from the unburying of her ancestors, she placed Momma's sadness at her back and climbed down the tree.

She stole back through the woods. Buoyed by the magic, her flight to her house was silent and quick and numb. She had no more plans to enact, no more ugly ways to hurt her family and force them into a position they clearly didn't want.

There was only one option left to her.

She had to figure out how to stay.

"What're you doin'?" Nettle asked, her voice laced with the kind of irritation she reserved only for Sybaline or her sisters.

Sybaline spotted her through the trees right before Sybaline's house.

"I'm home all by my lonesome, with Marlys and Tevi already moved out, so I decide to go search for you. You know where I find you? At the graveyard. You know what I find you doing? Something sneaky! That's what."

"You're mad at me because I was doing something sneaky?"

"No! I'm mad because you were doing it without *me*."

"How should I have known you'd be interested in sabotaging the graveyard relocation!" Sybaline yelled, liking the way the words ripped out of her throat. Hollering was better than thinking about how bad she felt for nearly ruining the sad moment her momma and aunts had shared at the graveyard.

Nettle's eyes, too big for her face, grew wide. "Why would you go and do a fool thing like that?"

"I don't want to move. I'm *not* moving. I thought maybe if I stopped the graves from being dug up, our family would figure out how to stay."

Nettle snorted. "You know our aunties could've easily stopped your magic."

"It was a bad idea. I know it now."

"You were desperate," Nettle said, walking close, setting both hands on either side of Sybaline's face and squishing her cheeks. She grinned. "Usually I'm the one coming up with bad ideas, not you."

"Desperate times," Sybaline said, her cheeks squishing more as she tried to talk, making Nettle laugh. "Desperate measures!"

Nettle dropped her hands, her expression falling somber. "My momma decided to take the money from the government and keep it awhile, instead of spending it on a new house in the city. She's moving us to Granddaddy Neal's farm instead. That's where Marlys and Tevi are."

Sybaline's body went cold. It spread straight from her lungs and into her toes, freezing the soles of her feet. "But your Granddaddy Neal's farm is way far out! It's…it's—" Nettle's granddaddy owned cattle out in the mountains opposite the city. "I'm never going to see you again."

8

"You just said you aren't moving. If you stay here, you won't ever see me again anyway."

Sybaline went cold now for an altogether different reason. *I'm not moving*, she'd said, the truth of it coming from deep within her. She whispered, "Don't try to convince me to move. I couldn't bear it if you tried to convince me too."

"How are you going to stay? Everything's going to be underwater, and the last time I checked, you're not a fish."

Sybaline drew a slow breath through her nose, calming herself before saying, "I have magic."

"You're going to start transforming into a dandelion if you use the magic to stay."

"I don't see how saving the valley could be unnatural. It's got to be a good thing."

Nettle's gaze drifted off toward the treetops, as if she were thinking hard. "We could make sure to check every day to see if we're transforming."

"*We?* Oh no, Nettle. There's no 'we.' I'm not risking you in this!"

Nettle's hands shot to her hips. Arms akimbo and shoulders thrown back, she looked just like Auntie Wooline, all her sternness filling up Nettle's much smaller body. "*You* don't get to choose what I do. If you're staying, I'm staying. I don't want to move either. All the people who move change and forget about the magic. Look at your brothers. I don't want to turn out like them, forgetting who I was born to be."

Sybaline's chest seemed to expand, both hurting and feeling good at once. The relief that overtook her surprised her. She hadn't known she needed Nettle to stay until Nettle agreed.

"We've got a big problem, though, Syb."

"Our mommas," Sybaline said, already knowing what her cousin was thinking.

"We're gonna have to lie to both of them," Nettle said, face twisting. "Unfortunately, mine already knows not to believe me. She trusts you though. You'll have to convince your momma to let you come and stay with me at my Granddaddy Neal's, and you'll have to convince my momma to let me stay with you in the city. Our mommas are so busy, maybe they'll be distracted enough to believe us."

All the sickness and sorrow that Sybaline's body could possibly hold flooded her. She'd only just lied to Momma for the first time the other day. How could she already be making a habit of it?

"Desperate times," Nettle whispered.

Sybaline closed tight her eyes, tears rimming her lids and clinging to her lashes. The bare earth pressed up against her feet, holding her firm. "Desperate measures," she said back.

CHAPTER 10

"Can I stay with Nettle at her granddaddy Neal's? She invited me." In the space of just a few days, Sybaline had become a terrible daughter, making plans and telling lies and figuring out how to leave her family. This lie flowed from her easier than she would've thought. The ease of it told her she was making the right choice. Staying with the valley and her home was more important than anything else.

Momma's eyes, the same color as the sky when it dripped rain from invisible clouds, looked at her blank.

"Nettle and I were talking about the idea at her house earlier today. Auntie Wooline said it was all right. I could live there for a little while and help at the farm." Sybaline crossed her fingers behind her back, hoping Momma wouldn't have the chance to check her story with Auntie Wooline. Once Sybaline was at Granddaddy Neal's, Momma would have to send letters to check in on her; he didn't have a telephone. Letters were slow, and Sybaline could only hope they'd get lost in the mail.

In truth, Sybaline *had* been at the gristmill earlier, but she'd been there to lie to Auntie Wooline and ask if Nettle could stay in the city with her and Momma. Auntie Wooline had agreed, just so long as it was all right with Sybaline's momma.

"You want to go with them?" Momma asked.

It wasn't that Sybaline wanted to go; she wanted to *stay*. She said, "Yes," as certain as she could.

Momma turned away and looked at the house.

Sybaline rubbed her thumbs against her fingers while she waited; the soft scrape of calluses grating against one another filled the quiet day. Guilt churned inside her. "I'm sorry I asked—"

"Yes."

That simple word bore against the innards of Sybaline's ears, the tender skin that had popped the one time a tornado had passed through their valley. Even though this was the answer she needed, she fell apart on the inside at hearing Momma's *yes*.

Momma's yes was spoken without hardly moving her mouth. A yes that came low from the bottom of her lungs. A yes that held whispers of a no, but it was a yes nonetheless.

And that yes broke Sybaline.

The confusion of it ran through her, small rivulets that rushed along her veins and turned her insides into electricity. It *hurt*. She needed Momma to say yes, but part of her also needed Momma to say no. To tell Sybaline that she needed her daughter with her.

Sybaline forced herself to stand tall, her face not giving a single clue as to the turmoil that raged inside her, just like Momma would.

Here was the truth: The only thing Sybaline needed was the valley and the magic, and the valley and the magic needed her as well. They were tied together, and she had no other choice but to exist for it, even when everyone else had given up.

"Thank you," Sybaline said, then she ran to tell the news to Nettle—except when she bolted from her house, her feet took a strange route, ending at the bottom of the graveyard hill. Deep tire tracks marred the rain-softened earth. She tipped back to peer at the tips of Papaw's tree—what little of it she could see from the bottom of the incline, then she knelt and pressed her fingers into the dug-up soil.

Sybaline's family was leaving. Momma. Marlys and Tevi. Auntie Wooline and Aunt Ethel. Cedric and Benjamin had already gone. Everyone was leaving except for Papaw, though that was only because he didn't have a choice in the matter.

And Sybaline was running away from it all. Except, she wasn't running away. Not really. She was refusing to go.

"I'm staying here with you," Sybaline told Papaw, speaking her and Nettle's shameful plan aloud.

We always have a choice, Aunt Ethel had said. *There's a third choice. We can use our magic and stay.*

—————

Sybaline made a knapsack for herself, filling it with odds and ends she snuck from the trunks Cedric hadn't yet taken to the new apartment. Nettle did the same, bringing with her an assortment of goodies Sybaline would never have considered necessary: a pack of toothpicks, a needle and string for patching holes in their clothes, some old seeds she thought might could grow into apple trees.

"You'll see," Nettle said. "You're going to thank me for these things."

They stowed everything up in the branches of Papaw's tree, knowing their mommas and aunts had already said goodbye and wouldn't make the trip up the hill again. Sybaline slipped and slid down the hill, coming back from her last trip to stash away supplies when Momma appeared, standing at the bottom of the hill and leaning against a shady tree.

Sybaline's heart skittered up her spine and lodged itself in her throat.

"Been spending a lot of time saying goodbye to Papaw, Sybaline." Momma pushed herself away from the tree, coming out and into the sun. She shaded her eyes with one hand, peering up the hill to where Papaw's branches pointed toward the sky. "You know the top of that hill's the highest point inside the valley, higher even than town? If you want to reach higher elevation, you have to climb the mountains."

Momma held out her arms, and Sybaline walked into them, feeling the murmur of Momma's words in her chest in the same way she heard them in her ears.

"I'm proud of you." Momma tightened her hug. "This has been a difficult time, and you've weathered it well."

Sybaline's chest crumpled, shame collapsing the bone.

Momma held her at arm's length, moving so that she caught Sybaline's gaze. "Cedric and I will come pick you up from Wooline's during the holidays. I hope being with your cousins helps you adjust to being away from the valley."

Sybaline memorized all the creases in Momma's face. The gray hairs wisping her forehead. The dark rings lining the irises of her eyes. The harsh curves of her cheekbones. The sun kisses dotting the bridge of her nose. Sybaline whispered, "I don't want to leave you."

Momma took hold of Sybaline's face, fingertips light against her temple and jaw, and ran her thumbs over Sybaline's forehead. "Our lives were always meant to diverge at some point. It's how the world works. Be good for your auntie. I'm proud of you for being brave and willing to find home somewhere else."

Somewhere *here*, Sybaline thought. The truth gummed up the insides of Sybaline's mouth, making it impossible to say anything else.

The brisk chill of the fall world nipped at Sybaline's earlobes as she walked beside Momma, and then, when Momma went up into the house, she kept on walking, not daring to turn back, not even when Momma called out, "You best be good to Wooline! You know I'll be sending letters to check in on you!"

Sybaline knew then that if she turned around, she might very well lose her nerve. Instead, she held tight to the knowledge the decision to stay was the only one she was capable of making.

By the direction Sybaline had left, Momma would think she were heading to Nettle's. Auntie Wooline was leaving today to drive to Granddaddy Neal's, while Momma wasn't leaving until tomorrow. Instead of following the overflowing creek that jutted across her family's land, and then crossing to the stream that led to the gristmill, she wound through the woods, circling back behind her house. Small curls of smoke cut up through the treetops, and she imagined Momma making one last dinnertime meal at the hearth. Pinching her eyes shut, she felt her way with her feet for a moment, collecting all her sorrow and then forcing herself not to glance back toward the lonely shape of her home.

Once at Papaw's hill, she dug her toes into the ground and her fingers into the dirt and propelled herself upward.

The graveyard was a tangled mess of shorn earth and upturned dirt. Despite all the minutes she and Nettle had spent sneaking up here, neither had time to smooth over the disturbed land from the grave relocation. Flowers no longer grew around the headstones marking plots where people had been buried, but instead were marked by crumpled petals and torn roots and stems snapped in half. The cemetery was devoid of her family, all except for Pawpaw's tree. She felt the emptiness of it in the strange way magic flowed through the earth, not forming small hiccups of warmth beside each body inside their caskets.

Sybaline righted the earth around the graveyard while waiting and watching as the sun crept across the sky. She wanted to grow the grass fresh and plant new flowers, but if she did, Momma might very well feel her using magic and come to investigate. She couldn't risk it.

At some point, Nettle arrived, and Sybaline understood that if Nettle was here, it meant Auntie Wooline had left. Nettle's plan had been to watch her momma drive off and then make the walk to Sybaline's.

"No turning back now." Nettle slung off the pack she carried and laid it at Papaw's feet: the last of the supplies they'd been able to gather. "How was it leaving your momma?"

"All right," Sybaline lied.

"It was all right for me too."

Sybaline glanced up, finding the same lie she'd just told in Nettle's face. It hadn't been *all right* for either of them, but that didn't mean they had to talk about it.

Nettle cleared her throat and then knelt in the grass, helping to make right what the government workers had done to the burial ground.

When at last night fell, they climbed between the mounding roots of Papaw's tree and settled into a cozy hollow, curling against each other and pulling tight over their shoulders one of the blankets they'd packed.

They didn't speak. What else was there to say?

CHAPTER 11

The next day, Cedric came. The grumble of his borrowed truck cut through the birdsong of the valley, interrupting their melodies. Sybaline and Nettle were up in Papaw's branches, looking out over the valley, the trees below shedding leaves as the earth made its way through fall.

Cedric must've never turned off the truck; the growl of the engine never stopped. He loaded up the last trunks and loaded up Momma, because soon enough, the rumbling echo pulled away from the direction of Sybaline's house and moved the forest, heading toward the city.

Nettle handed Sybaline a wedge of cheese and a chunk of cornbread as they watched. Sybaline took it but found she couldn't eat. She was crying too hard. More tears than Sybaline would have known her eyes held fell down her cheeks and flowed over her chin. She didn't bother wiping them away because she knew it would be pointless. More would replace them.

"I can want two things at once," Sybaline said. "I want to be here, and I also want to be with my momma."

"I miss mine too," Nettle said, and Sybaline realized her cousin was crying as well.

They were the soft type of tears, ones that were too big for their bodies to hold, but not ones that dragged out their innards to the outer world. Sybaline had only sobbed like that once, and it had been when Poppa had gotten his summons for war. She'd had a headache for days after that sort of crying. This sort felt like washing herself of sorrow— that when the tears ended, she would feel better, instead of worse.

After a time, tears stopped blurring her vision, and when they did, light bathed the whole wide world in what Tevi would have called starlight. Sometimes after it rained, the valley turned into a sparkling field, water beading on leaves and reflecting back the sky. It could be difficult to look at, the beauty and brightness of it too much for the eyes.

"We're going to have to do something about the water," Nettle said, interrupting Sybaline's thoughts.

Sybaline blinked and rubbed away the last of the tears that dampened her lids. When she did, it was to notice that the sparkles below were from the peculiar way in which water now collected on the earth. Light glimmered against water puddling among the grass below. She said, "Sheriff told us this part of the valley would flood sooner than anywhere else."

"First order of business." Nettle held up one finger. "Stop your home from flooding."

Sybaline and Nettle didn't waste time. They carted their belongings from Papaw's tree to Sybaline's house and dumped them before the hearth; they'd have to spend time making things feel homey later on. Right now, they couldn't focus on the barren shelves or the stone fireplace empty of ashes or the cast-iron cook stove Momma hadn't been able to take with her.

Nettle crouched in front of Sybaline's porch. Before her, water shimmered between the grass, forming a thin sheet, still enough that had it frozen over, they could have slipped around the trees and around her house with their boots on. She said, "This is the strangest thing I've ever seen in my entire life. What's the plan, Sybaline? How do we stop the water?"

"I've been thinking—"

"I'm so proud of you! Thinking is a good thing to do."

"And I'm pretty sure we need to build a wall of water."

Nettle looked up, doubt lining her eyes and wiping away the silly grin she'd worn a moment before.

"Benjamin reminded me about the fire, about how Aunt Ethel built that wall of flames that held back the wildfire. She made a little hole in the center of the fire for us to stay safe in. We could do that with water—build a wall to hold the lake back."

"Remember that Aunt Ethel started growing vines all over her because of that?"

"She was trying to save us, which I suppose is an unnatural use of magic. If we're trying to save the *valley*, that's got to be good."

"The valley isn't some sentient thing, deciding what a good use and a bad use of magic is."

"That might be true, but you *know* our mommas have always told us not to use magic selfishly. This isn't selfish of us."

Nettle nodded, some of her doubt disappearing. "You make a good point."

"Besides," Sybaline said, looking out over her family's land, "I can't think of a single other idea."

It felt like a century ago that Sybaline's little cousins had played with their magic, camouflaging themselves with creek water. Now, Sybaline and Nettle used the same technique of manipulating the natural world to build their wall.

They sat on the front porch, and they *pushed*. Smidgens of water peeled up from the grass and rolled back, forming a small wave as it gathered and receded from her home. Sybaline stood and ran after the water, watching as the wave grew in height and drew away into the forest.

"Don't push the water out of the creek. We'll need fresh water still." Nettle ran behind her. "We have to make sure we don't stop the spring from flowing."

Sybaline could feel Nettle working magic beside her as they ran, and so she *pushed* harder. The water continued to flow away, drawing up and over the creek while still allowing the natural spring to flow. On the other bank, the wave stopped and churned in place, forming a tiny wall, just inches high.

She sat and dunked her feet into the creek, asking, "Are we okay with building the wall here? Once the water rises, we won't be able to get to anything beyond the creek."

Nettle sat beside her. "It would take even more magic to push the water out farther. I think we should focus on the places we need to save."

Sybaline agreed, and so this was the place they stopped pushing back the water. The lake would keep rising and the rest of the valley would flood, but her home would be saved. They sat and watched for a while, wanting to see their wall work, but the flooding of the valley was too slow to truly notice the water creep higher.

"I'm bored," Nettle said.

"So am I." Sybaline climbed to her feet and turned to walk

along the wall. They'd built it *here*, but she wanted to see what it looked like elsewhere.

Together, they hiked beside the inches-high wall. It rose on the opposite side of the creek and led along the bank, cutting across it when they came to the place where Nettle's family's land began. The small wall then flowed from the creek and bisected the stream that funneled to the waterwheel, circling around the whole gristmill and continuing north. On and on they walked, heading along a path that wound in a huge circle until it ended back at the creek.

They'd walked in a giant ring with Sybaline's house at its center.

"It's like a wall that goes around a castle," Sybaline said.

"Tevi would like that," Nettle said.

"She'd like it even better if there were battlements and a moat around the wall."

Nettle laughed. "The *lake* is going to be like a moat."

"We did good work today." Sybaline made her way back home, realizing then just how tired her body was. "I feel very good about this choice of ours."

<hr>

Sybaline woke in the middle of the night, fear collapsing her innards. A nightmare had filled up her head—their wall of water caving beneath the pressure of the flooding waters. Even now, she knew that she and Nettle could decide to leave. To go. To step over the wall and walk along the soggy valley floor, taking them away from the magic altogether.

But even as the option slid through her head, it slid right back out again. She wouldn't—*couldn't*—make the choice to leave. She'd committed to the course. She'd set herself to saving what she could of the valley, to saving *herself.*

With her magic, she pushed and pushed, desperately reinforcing the water wall as best she could.

With the magic, she was making it so they had to stay.

CHAPTER 12

Two weeks after creating their wall of water, she sat on the bank of the river and washed clean her feet of the mud caked along her toes. A bucket sat beside her, filled to the brim with water.

"See, you're glad now that I saved us a bucket. Told you we'd need one," Nettle had said when they'd first headed to the creek to gather drinking water.

She gazed out at the silty wall that rose on the opposite side of the creek. Before, the water had only been inches high, but now, it crawled up and over the trees. It was as if the flooding lake was pressed flat against a pane of glass. It was pretty, in a strange sort of way. Sometimes, if she watched hard enough, she saw movement on the other side—fish swimming past.

The lake had inched up her barrier, lapping gently against the wall. She reached for the warmth of the magic then, but quickly pulled away: she and Nettle had agreed not to use it for anything else, just in case it detracted somehow from the magic that was being used to hold up their wall.

If she reached for it now and tugged it away, the water might come flooding down. It would swallow her whole. Standing, she grabbed up the handles of the bucket and lugged it through the woods, heading toward home.

"The water wall is almost over the treetops," she reported to Nettle, who sat on the front porch, working on small traps for catching rabbits or squirrels. "And this is drinking water, *not* washing water."

"How was I supposed to know?" Nettle muttered, referring to their first days inside their castle fortress when she'd washed her hands in the drinking bucket before dinner.

"You know now." Sybaline carted the bucket inside and set it in the kitchen. She looked through each of the contents they'd managed to keep with them, and decided she'd make cornbread to go with the rabbit Nettle would bring back after checking the traps she'd laid earlier in the week. To make cornbread though, she'd need to pick corn and grind it down, and *that* would be difficult, seeing as how Momma had the handheld mill. The task would be time-consuming and tiring, but there was nothing for it except to get it done.

In the garden, memories of Momma lingered among the plants: in the flower boxes filled with lettuce, in the blueberry and raspberry bushes, in the cherry trees and peach trees, in the tall tomato plants, and in the stalks of corn.

"Hello, pumpkins," she said.

"Well done growing," she told the beans.

"Keep up the good work," she said as she petted the branches of her mother's apple trees.

She did the garden work by hand and didn't use one single bit of magic. No matter how much she missed its comfort, she told herself to be good.

In the next days, Nettle and she would have to work nonstop to pick what foods grew in fall and figure out how to can it for the winter. They'd managed to sneak away some of the items their mommas had canned, like the strawberry rhubarb jam they'd eat with cornbread tonight, but they'd have to make more of their own to survive the winter. This meant they'd have to go through the eleven hills of pumpkins Sybaline's momma planted, boil the pumpkins up, and figure out how to preserve them. They'd eat squash for months.

For the cornbread, Sybaline chose corn that was ready to be picked and turned into flour, its husks all papery and dry, cracking off in her hands. She picked and picked, tying the stalks on a line that she'd hang from the kitchen to let dry. This corn would feed them for months, too, and she was thankful for Momma's work in growing it. Using a stone bowl and a rock, she set to work turning the corn into meal. By the time she was done, her whole body cramped, and she wanted to cry from the work of it, but at least she was done.

At least they'd have good food to eat—

"We've got a problem," Nettle said from the doorway. Her hands were empty, not holding the rabbit they'd wanted to eat for dinner. "Something's scared off all the animals. Either that or all the bunnies got stuck on the other side of the water wall. All the traps were empty."

"Nothing's here except for us to scare away bunnies. We'd have noticed if a fox or coyote were around." Sybaline dumped her cornbread mixture into the cast-iron skillet Nettle had snuck from Auntie Wooline and slid it into the stove. "And I doubt *all* the rabbits got stuck on the other side of the wall. Maybe when you check the northern traps tomorrow, you'll find a rabbit. Or your squirrel traps. They're bound to catch something. Squirrels can still climb over the wall and live in the tops of the trees; it's not like they'd get stuck on the ground like the bunnies would."

"Good ole tree rats." Nettle pressed her back into a wall and slid down it until she sat. "Some days you don't catch anything, and that's okay. I sure don't like it, though, and I'm *tired.*"

"Yeah well, my arms have been cramping all afternoon from this cornbread making."

"Woe is you."

Sybaline laughed and shook the one cooking towel she'd kept from Momma at Nettle. Later, they ate dinner on the front porch, rationing the cornbread so they'd have some left for the morning.

Evening drew its curtains closed over the day, darkening the skyline. Sybaline loved this moment, when the day suddenly lengthened. There was too much work to do when the sun was out, and so now, when she finally had the chance, she crept to the grass, kicked up her feet, and peered at the stars that speckled the sky.

She watched them blink into existence. Though, as they did, a growing sense of strangeness filled her, as if the world had gone off kilter somehow. Her brows knit together, tightening as tension ran through her body.

"Something's wrong," she whispered, though Nettle didn't hear, for she was up on the porch playing a funky rhythm with the two spoons they had. Unease spread through her, and she hollered, "Hush, Nettle! Please!"

Startled, Nettle popped her head up. Her hands and the spoons froze midair.

Sybaline identified what was wrong then. "Why's it so quiet?"

Silence stretched between the trees and filled her front yard. No bullfrogs or cicadas or buzzing insects bullied their way against one another, padding the woods with their frenzied songs. This silence reminded her of when she'd ventured into the rock quarry when she was a kid and had stood too close to an explosion. The world had zipped quiet afterward, and she'd patted her ears, thinking they'd stopped working altogether.

Sybaline shivered, a small tremor running through her muscles without her control. "You know what I noticed earlier in the garden? There weren't any animal tracks."

Nettle looked at her, sharp. Both their mommas had a heck of a time keeping all the wild animals away from their crops. There were always tracks that crossed through the yard: raccoons and deer and rabbits and mice.

"Maybe something scared them away," Nettle said.

"Maybe they all got stuck on the other side of the water wall." Sybaline closed her eyes and listened hard. A small sound came to her then: the swish of water as it hugged the bark of the trees, climbing up and up toward the clouds.

Opening her eyes, she peered toward the skyline, imagining the point where their water wall might now have risen above the treetops. In that moment, it didn't remind her so much of a simple wall, but perhaps instead of a mouth, hungry and held open, waiting for them to step between its teeth into the darkness beyond.

CHAPTER 13

Nearly one month after they'd decided to stay, the last birds in the valley took flight in the morning. They puffed into the sky, wings beating hard and breaking the quiet that had muffled the world the night before. They weren't warblers or sparrows or any of the wintering birds that flew south for the cold season, but instead were ones that should have kept their roosts year-round.

The birds parted with the valley, and Nettle said mournfully, "I guess we won't hear birdsong again."

Sybaline sat in the grass with her boots beside her, hating that she was considering lacing them up over her feet. She'd scrubbed them raw early that morning with the last of their drinking water, checking over every inch of her skin. Her toes were *cold*, and she couldn't find a reason for it.

"I'm not turning tree," she said to her boots, as she shoved her numb feet inside the leather. "Not a tree or a vine or a flower or a root or even a pigweed."

"What are you talking to yourself about?" Nettle asked as she came down the porch steps, a fishing line dangling from her hands. "And *why* are you putting on your boots? Don't you dare tell me that government man got to you with his *you'll even be able to buy shoes* comment."

"My feet'er cold, is all." Sybaline tied the laces into a bow, then tucked the loops behind the tongue to make sure they wouldn't come undone.

"Huh," Nettle said, sounding unconvinced. "I'm going to go check the traps in the north. Cross your fingers that we snag ourselves a fat rabbit for dinner."

"I'm going to go fetch more water."

"I was hoping you'd say that." Nettle held out the fishing line. "Catch a fish while you're out by the creek, will you?"

Taking her supplies, Sybaline trekked across the yard and into the tree line, shivering as a chill worked its way over her arms just as soon as she was out of view of the sun. She widened her eyes, pausing for a moment to let her vision adjust to the shadows. Her feet knew the right way to walk, even if they were in boots, so after a moment, she continued again on the path to the creek.

The shadows of the woods intensified as she drew closer, the world resembling a moonlit night rather than full day.

Uncertainty tightened her shoulders. "You're not scared,"

she told herself, shaking loose the tension. "You're just unsettled. Nobody in the history of ever has liked scary shadows."

Moving slow around the trees, she headed in what she knew was the right direction. The closer she drew, the deeper the darkness became, until she couldn't quite see her booted feet moving over the path when she looked down. The rhythms of the creek came through the woods, a happy sound that to Sybaline's ears, sounded like her valley, except when she reached it, it looked nothing like her valley, because it looked like nothing at all.

Darkness wrapped itself over the creek, cast down by the towering wall of water on the opposite bank. Craning her neck back, she peered through the treetops that had filtered sunshine two days before. Now, the sky was lost to a black slate.

"What's happening?" she asked. It was as if the wall of water had started to form a roof overhead, closing out the sky.

Clutching the handle of her bucket, she dipped it into the creek. With it full, she gently set it on the ground, then leaned forward to drink as much as her stomach could hold.

Careful now, she gathered the bucket and took tiny steps to orient her body in the direction of her house. She scanned the forest for smidgens of light she'd hoped would sneak through the edge of the forest and the place where sunshine existed, but no, the sun didn't stretch this far.

Never in her life had she walked so slow as she did now.

She tested each step with her toes before putting her full weight on her feet. The water in her arms strained her muscles and blossomed aches in her shoulders. Her feet bumped into the wide roots of a tree, and she paused. She didn't remember this tree, didn't remember it from the past or from the walk to the creek just minutes before. She had no idea where she was. Inching her toes along the ground, she felt at the roots and allowed it to lead her to the trunk of the tree.

"Oh!" Sybaline said, exhaling hard and realizing she did indeed know her location. "I know you, Mr. Walnut Tree."

Relieved, she stepped over the root and landed straight on a fallen walnut. The round bulb rolled from beneath her foot, sliding against the sole of her boot. She clutched the water bucket, throwing out an arm to catch hold of something to stop her fall. Grasping at a tree limb, her hand scraped against the wood, slowing her weight as she dropped to her knees. Water slopped over the edge of her bucket, soaking her sleeve and disappearing into the dirt and wetting her boots.

Forcing herself to stand again, Sybaline looked up. It was habit; looking *up* to find the sun was habit, but as soon as she did, a sob came from her chest, because all that hung above her was heavy blackness.

Sudden fear coursed through her. She wanted the sky and the sun and the wind, and without thought, she ran. Dragging

her half-full bucket with her, she escaped down the path on a
wild tilt toward the place she knew light existed.

———————

"I swear to you, there's a bear living in the woods." Nettle
paced the front yard, wearing a path through the grass. "We
got cursed cause of that boy's dumb ole teddy bear comment,
I know it."

Sybaline set the bucket on the ground and then placed
her hands on her knees while she caught her breath.

"I wanted to check the northern traps, right? I decided
on my way north I'd take a nice long walk by the gristmill to
see my home, but you know what I found when I went that
way? Total destruction! The front yard was a mess. All sorts
of random things were piled up on the porch, like twigs and
logs and leaves. A bear probably found our front door open
and decided it'd make a nice cave to hole up in for the winter!"
Tossing up her arms, Nettle turned toward Sybaline but then
froze and said, "What's got you so bothered?"

"Oh," Sybaline panted, still trying to calm her heart. "Oh,
nothing, just the fact that our water wall has gone and decided
to make itself a *roof*."

"What?"

"You heard me! It's turned over on itself. It's crawling over

109

the trees. The whole forest is completely dark. I couldn't see the creek at *all* when I got there!"

"Did you fish?"

"*What?* No! No...I—" Sybaline had no memory of the fishing line. She knew she'd carried it with her toward the creek, but she also knew she hadn't carried it back with her. "I think I lost it."

"That was our only fishing pole!"

"It was dark!"

"It's dark half our lives! I know for a fact this isn't the first time you've been in the woods in the dark."

Sybaline growled, feeling a lot like how Tevi must feel when she wanted to tackle Marlys. "And if a bear's living in the gristmill, we sure aren't going back there again."

Nettle's mouth parted, eyes growing wide and sad. Sybaline hated that expression on her cousin's face.

"I'm sorry. I didn't mean we wouldn't go back to the gristmill. We'll go back. We won't make you say goodbye to your home."

Nodding slow, Nettle said, "I'm sorry I wasn't listening about the woods and the...water wall roof." Her lips twitched, and then all of sudden, she laughed hard, snorting out her nose.

"It's not funny!" Sybaline said, except that the harder Nettle laughed, the more she wanted to laugh, too, all the fear in her turning into relief. It poured out of her, and she collapsed into Nettle's arms when her cousin came near.

They made their way back to the porch and sat on the top step, trying and failing to calm down. Small laughs kept sneaking out of them.

"We could kill the bear and eat it," Nettle said.

"Your daddy did the hunting, Nettle. All we know how to do is set traps and fish."

"We can figure it out."

"How? What are we going to do...whittle ourselves a couple of spears and chase it down?"

Nettle shifted, uncomfortable, not laughing anymore.

Sybaline couldn't picture herself up against a bear.

"What are we going to do about the water wall roof?" Nettle asked.

Sybaline set her elbows on her knees and her chin in her hands, peering toward the tops of the trees, then in a rush, she stood, latched her arms around one of the posts to the porch overhang, and demanded, "Boost me up!" Without hesitation, her cousin grabbed hold of her flailing legs and helped push. She snatched hold of the lip of the roof and heaved up, feeling awful bad when one of her boots connected hard with one of Nettle's hands.

Scrambling onto the overhang, she didn't stop there, but

stooped low and crawled to the highest point of the roof. She'd never been here before, though she remembered Benjamin sneaking up a time or two. Once at the top, she turned and looked over the horizon.

"What is it?" Nettle called. "What do you see?"

The breath stilled in Sybaline's chest, her lungs forgetting how to inflate. The wall of water wasn't quite like a wall anymore, but instead was shaped in a giant curve. It was like a glass bowl had been flipped upside down and placed over the land with Sybaline's house protected beneath it. Water lined the edge of the bowl, pressing against its top. It wouldn't take long until every inch of it were covered over.

"How bad is it, Sybaline?"

"Real bad, Nettle." Sybaline clambered back down the roof, trying not to fall in her haste, but the truth was that she couldn't waste time.

The truth was, they only had days to prepare before the sun disappeared altogether, casting them in complete darkness.

CHAPTER 14

Sybaline lay on their makeshift bed in front of the fireplace. "I thought we were only making a wall. We made the wall, that was it! It wasn't supposed to have a roof. The sky was always supposed be visible."

"We must've made a mistake." Nettle lay beside Sybaline, her hands folded over her tummy.

"How could we have made a mistake while making a *wall*?"

Nettle drummed her fingers against one another. "Maybe we didn't make a wall. If it has a roof or a top, it can't just be a wall."

"What else could we have made? A…a dome? A glass bowl?" she said, remembering what it'd looked like from her house's roof.

"I don't know, Syb." Nettle sighed and turned over under her blankets. "Maybe we made a bubble. A giant air bubble that we'll live inside. The lake will slide right over top of it."

A tremor tightened Sybaline's skin, her mind not liking the thought of a giant, invisible bubble stretching above them.

The flames of the fire she'd built earlier heated her feet, and she wiggled her toes. For the first time in days, they weren't chilled to the bone. She'd taken her boots off and had placed them beside the hearth, so they'd be snugly warm to slide into in the morning. Thinking about warm boots, she fell asleep, not letting herself contemplate the sky or the wall or the water, only being grateful that she was in her home with Nettle.

When they woke in the morning, the outside world shone a shade of gray Sybaline associated with the evening. She rubbed her eyes and squinted out the window, wondering if she'd woken earlier than normal.

"Lazy sun," she said, and opened the front door. Stepping down the porch, she made her way into the yard and checked for the sun in the east. There, she should be able to see its rays peeking over the tippy-tops of the mountains, but...

"Nettle? *Nettle!*" she hollered. Clatters and bumps came from inside the house, and Nettle stumbled out, hair flying uncontrolled around her head.

"What? What's happened? Where's the bear?" Nettle stumbled down the steps, looking as if she were still half asleep.

"There's no bear... What's with you and bears?" Sybaline pointed up and then drew a big circle around the sky. "*Look.*"

When Nettle tipped her head back, the entire set of her body shifted. All the sleepiness from her face drifted away, her expression solidifying into one that was lined with unexpected anger. Seeing for herself what had so scared Sybaline, she murmured, "I didn't think it'd happen this fast."

It looked like they were protected from the lake by a bubble now instead of by a simple wall; Nettle had been right. A fine layer of sediment swum inside the water that covered most of the sky. Only a perfect circle hung above them, which revealed the clouds beyond. As the valley continued filling, the water levels would keep rising; soon, their bubble would cover over entirely and trap them inside.

"We're going to lose sight of the sun," Nettle said. "We're not going to have any light."

Sybaline's stomach seemed to drop out of her. "We need… we need to chop more wood to make fires, and…and—" She struggled to think of what exactly they needed to do to prepare for life without the sun.

"We need to find lanterns. We only have one. Lanterns and candles, and—" Nettle kept talking, but Sybaline stopped listening. She bolted.

She ran around the house, circling to a small door that led to the crawl space beneath the house. On her hands, she inched into the three-foot-high space beneath the floorboards.

The stone foundation of their home formed a giant rectangle around her. Blinking, she felt around, hoping not to tangle her fingers into the homes of the small animals that might live there. Her hand smacked into something hard and she closed around it, feeling at its edges—a...broken fork. She snuck it into the pocket of her dress, just in case, and kept searching. She picked up several odds and ends, and eventually came to a lantern that had a busted bottom. Nettle had broken it years before when they were playing, and instead of admitting it to Sybaline's momma, she'd hidden it.

Coming out from under the house, she ran to the front with the lantern held aloft. There, she found Nettle with her empty pack slung over her shoulder and the axe they'd swiped from Nettle's dad gripped in both hands.

"Remember the tree in front of the gristmill my momma strung lanterns onto?" Nettle tightened her hold on the axe handle, skin making a squeaking sort of sound as it rubbed against the well-worn wood. "There are three of them. They're little miniature things, but they work. Momma didn't pry them loose of the wood that grew around them before moving."

"We can't go to the gristmill. You said a bear's living there."

"We don't have a choice. We need those lanterns more than the bear does. We'll be quiet about it, and if the bear is gone, it means we can search the gristmill for anything we might could use."

Sybaline ran inside the house, shoved her cold feet into her boots, and ran back out again, following swift after Nettle. Her cousin walked with shoulders tossed back and hair bobbing in a halo.

The trail they usually took was too dark, too shadowed by the encroaching water above, and so the snaking path Nettle walked them along was one they'd rarely blazed before. Kudzu and brambles blocked their walk, and they had to use the axe to clear a path more than once. Scrapes spotted Sybaline's hand, thorns snagging her skin as she shoved aside bushes to make way for her feet. The temperature dropped as they paved their way through, a thin layer of water blocking the sky from their view. It reminded Sybaline of when she swam and opened her eyes beneath the water, sunlight warping as it pushed through the liquid. By the time they made it to the cleared-out land surrounding the gristmill, they had come to a place where the water above must have been half a foot thick, for deep shadows cast the gristmill in darkness.

"I'm so sweaty," Nettle whispered, panting a little as she clutched at the axe. "How can it be so chilly here, and I still be so sweaty?"

Sybaline wiped her own face off with her sleeve. Nettle was

right; the walk had made sweat drip down her spine, sticking the back of her dress to her skin.

They inched forward through the dark, making their way to the lantern tree more out of memory than from sight. The tree itself stood in front of the gristmill and was one Auntie Wooline liked to string up with decorations depending on the season. The lanterns had been hung one winter years and years before and tree bark had grown over their handles, lodging them in place.

Reaching the tree, Sybaline watched Nettle's form as she set the axe on the ground and rested the handle against the trunk.

Panic rose in Sybaline. She whispered, "Don't put it down. We might lose it."

"I'm not going to forget where I lay it."

That didn't comfort Sybaline; she could hardly see the axe through the darkness, even knowing exactly where Nettle had put it.

Nettle shifted beside her, hands reaching up and feeling along the tree branch above them. "Got it," she said, when she reached the lantern handle. The sound of scratches came as she peeled at the bark, whittling away at it using a small knife she'd carried along. This would be a good task for magic, but they'd long since decided *not* to use it unless they were desperate; they needed the magic focused on holding up the wall—the *bubble*.

"Hurry up," Sybaline said. Prickles ran along her back, the sweat on her skin cooling the longer they stood still. She turned, peering at the darkness and the quiet around them. It pushed against her, weighing her down, not unlike the thick quilts Granny Alminy had made. Those quilts, though, had comforted her; this suffocated. She murmured, "*Hurry.*"

"I *am* hurrying. You try doing this in the dark while standing on your tippy toes and attempting not to cut your fingers off."

"I just don't want the bear to come along, is all," she said, using the bear as an excuse: this darkness was not something she wanted to live inside, and she desperately wanted to race back to the sunshine that still existed over her house.

The crack of a twig came from their left, and Sybaline snapped her head in that direction. She reached out for Nettle but stopped before bumping her; she didn't want to rattle Nettle in her work and make her slice her skin instead of tree bark. The floorboards of the gristmill creaked, something large pushing its weight against the wood and making the whole house echo through with groans.

"The bear's in your house," Sybaline whispered.

Beside her, Nettle worked faster. The lantern came free

of the branch with a jolt. The clang of the handle falling to whack against the iron body made Sybaline flinch. She grabbed the lantern from Nettle, while Nettle went to find the next one.

Another groan split the air; the gristmill protesting something's weight as it moved across the central room.

"It's coming." Sybaline shifted so she stood on Nettle's other side, right between the house and her cousin's body. Everything inside Sybaline tensed, muscles drawing taut. She knew stories of people who'd been mauled by bears. They rarely survived.

The buzz of magic split the air as Nettle used it to crack open the tree branch. The lantern rattled, and it dropped into Nettle's hands.

"Got it! *Go, go!*" Nettle whispered. They'd only rescued two lanterns; the other one would have to stay behind.

Sybaline snatched up the axe, determined not to lose it in the dark as she'd done with the fishing pole.

They ran, closing the distance to the tree line and the path they'd carved on their way there. Behind them, a bang erupted, something big striking the innards of the house— sounding just like a door being shoved open and slamming into a wall.

Sybaline couldn't look behind her to find the bear

through the dark. All she could do was pay close attention to where she placed her feet, fear shooting adrenaline through her whole body.

Before her, Nettle grabbed up magic, pulling it straight out of the ground. Fear shot through Sybaline, as the path in front of them opened and all the roots and shrubs that had blocked their path cleared away in a hurry.

"We're not supposed to use magic!" she yelled and glanced above, hoping they weren't on the verge of being drowned because of Nettle's choice.

They bolted through the slot. Magic warmed behind them; Nettle worked to close the path and stop the bear from coming through.

Rattles and stomps sounded behind them, panting snuffles and breaths; the bear heaving its way through the woods, coming after them.

Sybaline stopped and turned, her chest caving in from the force of the fear that paved its way through her body. She dropped the axe and grabbed at the magic, taking it up by the handfuls, drawing it to her exactly how Aunt Ethel had done when she'd made the wall of fire to save them: desperately.

She imagined in her mind another wall, this one drawing from the water beneath them that ran through the earth below. She pushed and pushed, the dirt and land shifting and rumbling

121

in protest, as she stole water from the soil. A wall rose from the ground before them.

"Nettle?" came the smallest of voices. A high-pitched, mouselike voice, shivering straight through with fear.

Sybaline froze, her hands held in front of her, palms out. The magic continued working. Too much momentum had already been built for it to stop on its own.

"Nettle!" cried the person again.

Sybaline knew that voice, had heard that exact pitch before, when they'd hidden beneath her house in the crawl space when the tornado had rushed through the valley. Tevi had clutched at her and buried her head against her lap.

As brave as Tevi was, she didn't like surprises. She didn't like being scared, and right now, she was scared.

Through the shadows before her Tevi's outline appeared. She scurried through the woods, trying to lift her little legs high enough to climb over the bushes Nettle had drawn up behind them.

"Tevi?" Sybaline said.

Behind her, Nettle's footsteps stopped.

"Nettle!" shouted Sybaline's little cousin.

"*Tevi!*" Nettle screamed, just as the wall Sybaline had built shot straight into the sky, meeting with the edge of the bubble far above.

CHAPTER 15

Banging her fists against the wall that towered before them, Nettle screamed and screamed. It echoed through the quiet around them.

"It wasn't a doggone bear." She pounded at the wall. "It was my sister. Why was it my sister?"

"Bears don't use doors." Thinking back, Sybaline realized she'd heard the sound of the gristmill's front door being tossed open. She'd been in too much of a scared hurry at the time to think straight and hadn't understood it… There was no way a bear could open a door. She dropped her head into her hands.

"Make the wall go away," Nettle said, whipping around to face her. She whacked one palm into Sybaline's shoulder. "Make it *go away*."

Tentatively, Sybaline reached out and felt the wall she'd built, fingers meeting with a slick layer of water. She pushed, leaning against it, and then shoved *hard*. It didn't give, didn't shift, didn't move or let her through like the surface of a lake might. It was impenetrable, just like a layer of rock. Collecting magic to her, she tried to pull the wall down, but as she did, the bubble above them seemed to bend in—

"*Stop!*" Nettle grabbed Sybaline, and they both held their breath, looking up.

The bubble warped, then popped back into place, holding firm. If the bubble collapsed now, the lake above would collapse, too, and the water would flood in. They'd drown. *Tevi* would drown.

"We have to get to her," Nettle whispered, still staring at the place where the wall met with the bubble.

"Get to *them*," Sybaline said. "You know Tevi wouldn't be here without Marlys."

Nettle nodded, then bent and picked up the axe Sybaline had dropped. She turned and continued back to Sybaline's house. "If we can't go through the wall and we can't tear it down, we'll have to go around."

Inside her boots, Sybaline's feet ached fierce. The chill that had seeped into her bones spread into her ankles, and when they reached her house, she bent to rub the tender skin beneath the laces.

"Pack up all our supplies!" Nettle shouted as she stomped through the front door.

Sybaline stood upright. "What?"

"We're not coming back." Nettle's voice, muffled from inside the house, was nearly drowned out with the banging of the cast-iron fry pan against the stovetop.

"Why not?"

"If we get over there and we get my sisters, we're not coming back to your house."

Sybaline took quick steps up the porch, her hands fisting, clenching around the folds of her dress. "We've lived at my house this entire time. Why wouldn't we get Tevi and Marlys and come back here? Why would we move to yours, now?"

"My house has electricity!"

Sybaline deflated, shoulders turning concave. Of course— the gristmill had the stream and the waterwheel, and with the sky darkening overhead, they needed the source of light. Sybaline turned in a circle, cataloging all the memories from her life that were written into the boards of Papaw's house. At least if she were at Nettle's house, she was still in the valley. Surviving was much more important than being stubborn and trying to force her cousins to return here.

Sybaline went to the back of the house where a log pile was stacked up and dumped out the wheelbarrow they'd stashed beside it. She rolled it to the porch and set to filling it with all the supplies they'd be able to carry. Soon enough, it tottered high with the odds and ends they'd stowed away. They tied a blanket over the top and then a rope over that, ensuring nothing would spill out.

Nettle filled a lantern with a small amount of kerosene—they'd have to ration it—and held it up. Sybaline took hold of the handles of the barrow, and together, they plunged toward the woods and the path they normally walked. Too much had changed in a day. These woods were not the woods she'd grown up in. Quiet filled the forest. No breeze rustled the leaves or toyed with the stray hairs that fell from her braids, no animals scurried through the underbrush, no light bled through the crown of the trees above.

The world that had once been so full of life had turned into an in-between. Not alive and not dead, but something stuck betwixt the two.

Sybaline pushed the barrow over a bump, a sticky resistance tugging at the wheel. A pungent scent rose in the air. She shoved hard and rolled through the mess, knowing well the smell of rotten apples. In the woods were stray fruit trees, like the ones Momma had planted around their garden. The one she'd walked beneath must be dropping its fruit and leaving them to mold against the earth.

The farther they walked, the farther behind they left the circle of light. Shadows rolled over them, but Nettle didn't hesitate. She hurled herself along the path, lantern held low so as not to blind them and to shine light on the path their feet took. Soon enough, the only light was that of the lantern, no sunlight cutting through the black waters above.

Sybaline shivered in the darkness. The endless gloaming around them made the world a temperature she wished she had a coat to buffer against. Why hadn't she thought to keep warm, winter clothes?

Nettle walked in front of her, her free hand stretched out against the darkness, and then—*thwack*—she ran straight into a solid mass, her arm colliding with—

"The *wall*?" Nettle said, panic slipping into her voice. "You made the wall here?"

Sybaline's breath drew short. "No. I swear I didn't."

"Then why is there a wall?" Nettle held the lantern up and slid her arms over the expanse of the wall she'd discovered. Following it, she headed off trail where Sybaline couldn't follow with her barrow.

Thinking back, Sybaline did her best to remember what she'd done when she'd drawn water out of the earth and created the wall to stop the bear. She'd been desperate; she knew that much. She knew too that Momma always warned her against working magic when feeling intense emotion, be it anger or fear or joy. *It'll make you sloppy,* Momma said. Had Sybaline been sloppy?

Nettle crossed the path again, heading in the opposite direction, following the lines of the wall. Then all of a sudden, Nettle's light reappeared, "You raised walls everywhere, Sybaline. They curve all around. It's like a tunnel system."

Despair threaded through Sybaline. "I didn't mean to," she said beneath her breath, except in the quiet of the woods, her words sounded loud. "It was a mistake."

"There's nothing for it, Sybaline. We all make mistakes… This is a really bad one though." Nettle drew a hand down her face. "This part of the wall seems to curve around a ways down. We'll follow it and see if there's a way through. Let's go."

Nettle took them off the path, and Sybaline tried to follow, but of course, she couldn't follow with the wheelbarrow. It was too big and lumpy and couldn't cut over the thick shrubbery.

Gently, without looking back, Nettle tugged on the magic, and the undergrowth pulled away, leaving a trail the barrow could plow through. Sybaline found she couldn't complain or tell Nettle to stop. Every now and then, Nettle left Sybaline behind and picked her way through dense bushes to find where the wall stretched and curved. All the while, she did her best to point them in the direction of the gristmill.

As they walked, Nettle's breathing turned more and more ragged, and her hurried steps slowed to a creep. Sybaline watched the sagging shape of her shoulders and wished for a way to push energy into her cousin—Nettle had asked too much of herself today.

Sybaline glanced back in the direction of her home. "You're tired, Nettle. We need a break, and we need to sleep for the night. It's got to be night by now. We can start over in the morning."

"The morning won't come!"

"We've been at this for hours. You're going to collapse if you keep pushing yourself."

Nettle turned, slow, and raised the lantern. Light flooded the ground at Sybaline's feet. It crept up and up until it shone straight in her eyes. "My sisters are over there. They're at the gristmill, and they're in the dark. You saw that—they don't have the electricity up and running. If they did, they'd have had the lights on, and we would've known they weren't a bear."

"Your sisters are at the gristmill, and they're safe. They aren't going anywhere," Sybaline said with her eyes closed against the light. "They can take care of themselves."

"Marlys and Tevi can't take care of a mouse, much less themselves." Nettle's breathing still came in harsh gasps. Something was wrong with her cousin, and Sybaline knew it went beyond simply being tired.

Sybaline made the decision for both of them then. She turned, grabbing up a rough blanket from the wheelbarrow but leaving the actual barrow where it was, and headed in the direction of her house. Backtracking was much easier than paving the way; all they had to do was follow the clear path Nettle had opened.

In her front yard, the sky above was terribly dim. Evening light glowed against the clouds above and turned the world a shade of green gray she only saw when it was about to storm.

"It's harder being here than I thought it'd be," Nettle said, putting out their lantern and sitting on the ground with her arms wrapped around her knees.

Guilt rooted inside Sybaline. "You didn't have to stay with me."

"I couldn't let you stay alone."

Sybaline tipped her head back to look at the place the moon shone. The darkness of the lake crept overhead, inching and inching and *inhaling, exhaling* and gobbling up the gaps of sky still left to them. She felt at the magic and at the bubble above. When scared or nervous, she used to draw the magic close to herself for comfort, but not anymore. She couldn't afford to.

"It's harder being here than I thought it'd be," Nettle repeated, whispering now.

Darkness pressed in from all sides. It towered in the same way nightmares did in the middle of the night, looming inside Sybaline's mind and making her skin turn into prickles. She refused to look away from the still-open sky and at the walls of water surrounding them.

Sybaline breathed out through her nose and wiggled her toes inside her boots. They still ached, though it was a brittle sort of ache, not the sort that came after running hard through the woods. She stopped moving her feet against the earth and instead, used them to bring her up the stairs and into her home. She made a fire. She laid out the blankets. And when Nettle and she fell asleep, it was with the understanding that when they woke, the sky would be gone altogether, and they would have to find Marlys and Tevi without aid of the sun.

CHAPTER 16

Nettle slept. And slept…and slept, exhaustion seeming to not allow her to wake. Her fingers and toes fidgeted in her sleep.

Sybaline sat crisscross with her back pressed to Nettle, who lay on her side facing the fireplace. Golden coals gleamed amid the ash, streaks of light pushing delicate arms against the shadows inside the hearth. Sybaline turned away from this view and stared out the window opposite the fireplace. Her body told her it was time to be awake, despite the fact that no bands of sunlight filtered through the glass.

Curling up her legs, she shivered. All of her felt terribly cold, except for her feet that were too numb to feel much of anything at all. She pressed her thumb to patchy skin that ringed her ankles. There, she scratched at the dryness.

Nettle rolled over. Jumping, Sybaline pulled her socks up and turned to face her cousin.

"It got colder," Nettle said.

"The sun is officially gone." The windowpane showed

black, a slick covering of paint that dripped over the outside world.

Nettle rubbed her eyes, rustling the blanket that covered her. "I think Momma left some things in our house that couldn't be used anymore. Hopefully there are spare clothes. Otherwise, we're about to be wintry cold without the sun and without anything extra to wear. We're going to have to burn so much wood to keep the house warm."

Sybaline struck flint to set alight one of their lanterns. Light bloomed inside.

Nettle pushed to her feet, grabbing up the blanket and slinging it over her shoulders like a cape. "It's time to save my sisters."

They made a plan: they would head back to the creek and from there would retrace their steps, following the path Nettle had opened. This time as Nettle led, Sybaline opened herself to the magic, carving a path through the woods that the wheelbarrow could trudge along.

She'd never walked into so many trees in her life, and that was taking into account the time she, Nettle, Marlys, and Tevi played blindfolded tag in the woods. Even with the lanterns, she and Nettle kept getting turned around and confused and found themselves backtracking, having little idea in what direction they actually walked. Directions weren't so easy when their internal compass had nothing to give them assistance—no mountains, no sun, no outside world to tell them north from south.

The entire forest had become a backward place with Sybaline feeling as if she walked on the night sky but also somewhere far below, in some dark, unknown Neverland.

The valley had always breathed. It had murmured with wildlife: flowers stretching toward the sun, moonlight dimming as it filtered through the treetops, animals rustling through underbrush and calling to their families. The silence of the woods now was broken only by the sounds she and Nettle made. The only breathing that happened was caused by them, and it didn't feel so much like breathing as it felt like invading a place caught in a pause.

"I can't tell where we are," Sybaline said, trying to shake loose the sense that when that pause ended, something terrible would happen.

Nettle seemed just as confused as Sybaline, if her exclamations of "Squirrels chattering teeth!" and "Rat poo and froggy bottoms!" every time she stubbed her toe were anything to judge by. They stumbled through the shrouded world, until one point when Sybaline landed flat on her face after tripping over a tree root.

Sybaline groaned and clambered to her feet, right as Nettle began clapping. The sudden sound startled Sybaline.

"Listen." Nettle set down her lantern and clapped, turning in a slow circle as she did. "I thought at first that I was making it up, but I heard it when you fell. Listen."

Each clap of Nettle's vanished into the dark, sucked up by the blackness and the shadows and the arching trees that held their branches far over Sybaline's head in a canopy that was severed in half by the water.

Nettle clapped again, and then, Sybaline heard it.

"It's like Mr. Hollyfield's walking stick," she said, quiet, listening hard with eyes closed.

The echo of Nettle's claps came back to them, sharp and crisp, reminding Sybaline of the rock quarry on the opposite side of the valley, where sound bounced back and forth in waves.

But then, she took a step and then two more, searching for the echoes of sound. One of her numb feet turned sideways in a direction she wasn't looking, and her body went with it. She dropped down the side of an embankment, managing to let go of the wheelbarrow so it didn't smash on top of her. She slid down a small bank and landed with a bump in a patch of sand at the bottom.

"Oh!" Nettle held her lantern high and stepped up to the ridge Sybaline had fallen over. She shone the light over

Sybaline's prostrate form. "You found the stream to the water-wheel! Good job!"

"It wasn't on purpose, but thanks." Sybaline grasped her aching head and gingerly tested her ankles, but her ankles were as numb as her feet. She hoped they were in one piece.

"If this is the stream, it means we're almost to the gristmill…as long as you didn't make a wall across it." Nettle's voice *and* her light drew away, heading downstream, following the empty riverbed.

"Come back!" Picking up her own lantern that had been doused in the fall, Sybaline scrambled to her feet.

Nettle didn't wait, though, and she didn't slow. Instead, in her excitement, she disappeared fast around a bend.

Boots inching forward in the streambed, Sybaline tested her steps so as not to trip over any stones. She climbed up and over the bank to reach the path Nettle walked on, deciding not to search for where the wheelbarrow had landed. For a moment, she stayed on her hands and knees, taking in lungfuls of air that cleared her swimming head. Sunspots danced in her vision.

This darkness was complete. It was denser than *eyes closed at night*; than *blindfolded tag in the middle of the woods*; than *a tornado is coming, quick, beneath the house*; than *a nightmare holds you beneath water*; than *Freddy Applegate knows you have a crush on him and you want to die of embarrassment.*

Sybaline snapped her fingers beside her ears. The sound dampened against the harsh breathings of her own lungs. The depthless shadows snuck into the fibrous tissue of her body: the meat of her legs that cramped and bruised from the fall; the tubes of her veins, icy blood sliding through; her skin pulled taut with fear and cold. It pressed against her, and *into* her. It crept over her scalp and into her mouth, coating her teeth—

"What in ghostly dooms are you doing?" Nettle hollered from down the path. "Get up. We need to get to my sisters!"

Sybaline blinked, her vision fizzing and focusing on a small point of brightness—Nettle holding her lantern high, the warm gleam pouring over her head and tossing a long shadow made of wispy hair and strong shoulders. Sybaline climbed to her feet, limbs shaking, and stumbled down the path toward Nettle's light.

CHAPTER 17

No other walls stood in their path. The trek beside the empty stream felt as if it were an eternity long, each step they took passing over entire darkened worlds. Horrible thoughts danced through Sybaline's head: What if she'd built a wall behind Tevi as well as in front, and Tevi was now stuck inside a tunnel? What if Tevi and Marlys had left the gristmill to try and get to Sybaline's house? What if the girls were trapped somewhere in the dark?

She folded her hands together and wrenched on her fingers, praying her cousins remembered the most important rule of getting lost in the woods—*stay where you are; let those more experienced than you come find you.*

"Look," Nettle whispered. Her long strides paused, hiccupping, feet landing and pausing before picking up again.

Before them, a pinprick of light—the warm glow of a fire—broke the ongoing, everlasting darkness.

The sight of it tightened Sybaline's rib cage. She drew in shallow breaths.

Nettle bolted. She screamed, "Tevi! Marlys!"

Bang! The front door shot open, door handle smacking into the opposite outside wall. Sybaline couldn't count how many times Auntie Wooline had hollered at her daughters not to smack open the door.

Sybaline stood as witness, listening to her cousins' reunion—laughter and tears and at least one clattering thump as all three of them fell into a pile on the porch.

"Sybaline!" Nettle shouted, which was echoed by Marlys and Tevi yelling her name as well.

When Sybaline reached them, the relief that filled her buckled her knees and she sat down hard on the porch. Tevi toppled onto Sybaline's chest. She laughed and wrapped her arms around her little cousin.

It took a while, but Sybaline realized they all sat in the threshold of the front door, firelight spilling from the innards of the gristmill out onto the porch. The fire the girls had built raged inside the hearth.

"You're going to blaze through all your cut wood in a week if you keep the fire going like that," Sybaline said.

"It was dark," Tevi said. She and Sybaline sat huddled with their backs against the open front door, Tevi's face buried in Sybaline's shoulder.

"And cold," Marlys said.

Sybaline understood: the darker and colder it got, the higher they'd built the fire.

"I sure never much minded the dark before." Marlys leaned her own head against Nettle's shoulder. "I never minded it until the sun went away."

"Why are you here?" Nettle said. "I don't understand why you're not at Granddaddy Neal's."

"*You're* here," Tevi said. "*You're* not at Granddaddy Neal's."

Any words Sybaline could've said in response vanished from her mind. The sickening realization came to her that her little cousins had run away from home all because Sybaline and Nettle had stayed in the valley. Deep, unbearable guilt piled up in her. "You can't be here *only* because we're here."

"We got a letter from your momma, Sybaline," Marlys said. "Tevi opened it before our momma did. Yours was checking in on you. She asked if you were having a good time with us at our Granddaddy Neal's. But you *weren't* with us, and if you weren't with us and you weren't with your momma, you had to be somewhere else. We thought it meant that Nettle wasn't at your momma's like you said you'd be. You lied."

"We thought you were probably in the valley, and if you were in the valley, we wanted to be in the valley too," Tevi said.

"We made a plan then. Our parents was leaving us at Granddaddy Neal's and was going to Aunt Ethel's to help her settle into her new place. She'd be gone for weeks. We lied and told Granddaddy Neal we was going with Momma and Daddy, and then, we made a run for it."

"We came back to the valley!"

"But when we got to the gristmill, you weren't here."

"We stayed at Sybaline's," Nettle said.

Tevi's mouth formed an O.

"Why would you be at Sybaline's? The gristmill is bigger, *and* it has electricity," Marlys said. "Well… It'd have electricity if the water hadn't stopped running in the stream."

"We must've pushed out all the water from it when we made the water wall," Nettle said.

"*You* made the water wall?" Tevi asked. "We thought the valley made it."

"The valley can't make a water wall," Nettle said.

"It made sense to me." Tevi shrugged. "I don't like the valley as much without the sun."

Me neither, thought Sybaline, though she didn't dare speak the words aloud; she didn't like how they felt to hold in her mind.

Marlys and Tevi showed them around the gristmill and the little cocoon of blankets they'd piled before the fire to make a bed, telling them the story of how they'd arrived at the gristmill.

"The lake had already been rising," said Tevi. "We rowed a boat to get here."

"We only rowed it a little ways. As soon as we rowed far enough on top of the lake, our magic worked and we could use it to move across the water."

"That's *not* how magic's supposed to be used," Sybaline said out of habit.

"*You* built a water wall," Marlys pointed out.

Nettle snorted, covering her laugh with the back of one hand.

"But then, the boat came to this funny stopping point in the middle of the lake. We looked down, and there was a wall!" Tevi flung up her hands. "We pushed the boat right over the edge. It's probably in the woods somewhere now, not that we can find it in the dark."

All four of them huddled in the blanket pile together. Sybaline was awed at her cousins, knowing they'd probably hitchhiked all the way from their Granddaddy Neal's to the valley. There were so many ways things could have gone wrong for them, and the knowing of it didn't sit well in Sybaline.

Tevi yawned. She covered her mouth with one hand, but then through her fingers, she asked, "Why are *you* here?"

Sybaline shifted, discomfort rising inside her. She was in the valley because she hadn't wanted to learn a new way to live… and she was being forced to find a new way to live anyhow. She didn't know how to explain that to Tevi though.

Soon enough, her littlest cousins' breathing slowed. Both girls slept between Sybaline and Nettle, their warm bodies heating up the space beneath the blankets.

Sybaline stared at the ceiling where firelit shadows weaved across the wooden beams. She saw pictures there: a tiger, a foaming wave, an upside-down jellyfish. If only Tevi were awake to play the game with Sybaline, she'd probably see unicorns or dragons. As much as she liked Tevi, she didn't like her being here; it didn't feel safe.

You're here, Tevi had said. *You're not at Granddaddy Neal's... Why are you here?*

"Would you have stayed in the valley, if I hadn't stayed?" she asked Nettle. She knew deep in her gut she would have stayed at her family home no matter what, no matter if she was the only human being left down here. Staying had been the most important thing in the world to her.

Nettle didn't respond, though Sybaline knew she was awake, and in the silence she knew the truth: all three of her cousins were stuck beneath the lake because of her.

Morning arrived—or, Sybaline *assumed* morning arrived—and they all gathered on the front porch. Despite having snuggled against Tevi all night, a chill worked through Sybaline, burrowing into her feet and legs. She tried to hide her shivers, but Tevi glanced at her more than once. It didn't help either that they hadn't really eaten dinner the night before. Her tummy rumbled, distracting her.

"The problem is that we didn't think about keeping the water here running." Nettle tapped her fingers against her knees. "We need water moving through the stream to get the electricity to work in the gristmill, but we can't very well pull water from the lake. The whole bubble protecting us could collapse."

"I tried getting water out of the lake," Tevi said.

"*What?*" Nettle said.

"No, you didn't," Marlys said. "You tried to *fish* in the lake. You thought you could poke a net through the wall and catch yourself some fish." She paused, then added, "It didn't work."

"The wall was too hard. I couldn't get through it," Tevi said.

"We did too good of a job building the wall." Sybaline mourned. "If we can't make the waterwheel work, how are we supposed to get electricity? That was the entire point of staying at your house."

"We could always hook up wires to a potato," Nettle said. Then, at Sybaline's cross expression, added: "Just kidding. We don't have any potatoes…or wires."

"I need to eat." Sybaline scrubbed her fingers through her hair. "I can't think when I'm this hungry."

"Go pick something from my momma's garden."

Sybaline sighed and headed outside, wishing for her own momma and the hearty meals she used to make. She grabbed a lantern off the steps and walked onto the grass. The yard hadn't seen even a smidgen of rain fall from the sky recently...except the sole of her boot squelched into a paper-thin layer of water instead of crunchy grass. She stuck one finger into the dirt, fingers squelching into mud.

"Oh no, now what?" Sybaline said. "What's going wrong *now?*"

Wandering into the thick of Auntie Wooline's garden, she held her lantern low and examined a fat pumpkin that sat heavy in the dirt. The plants themselves looked healthy enough, but she couldn't get rid of the feeling that somehow, their roots were drowning inside the sludge.

She bypassed the plants and found an apple tree, picking two apples for each of them, and decided not to mention the water to Nettle... Maybe it would drain away.

"What we really need," Nettle said after Sybaline returned to the porch with the apples, "is a big ole pot to boil apples and make applesauce."

"You might could find one in town." Marlys wiped her

mouth where juice ran. "We'd have to bring lamps and stuff though—"

"It's real dark there," Tevi said.

Sybaline stopped eating her apple. "What do you mean... town?"

Marlys's brows drew together. "Town in the middle of the valley. You've been there loads of times."

Tevi said, "You already forgot about *town*?"

"Of course I haven't forgotten about town! It's just..." She turned to Nettle. "We walked the entire wall when we first made it. The bubble ends on the other side of the gristmill."

"It doesn't end," Marlys said, confused. "It reaches all across the valley. Tevi and I went there. The bubble goes all the way to the other side of town. We went there once, but then the water closed overhead, and it got too dark to explore."

Nettle stared at her sisters, then turned to Sybaline. "How is town beneath the bubble now, if it wasn't before?"

"I must've made another mistake." Sybaline rubbed her temples, remembering lying in bed at night, feeling desperately scared that the wall of water would collapse over them. She'd reinforced the magic, pushing and *pushing* at it... She must've pushed harder than she thought and had expanded the wall altogether, zipping it around other parts of the valley.

Nettle accepted Sybaline's simple explanation, saying,

"Syb, I think we should go now. We'll bring the lanterns and see what's left in town." She set her hand against the back of Marlys's neck. "Sybaline and I are going to go—"

"I want to go too!" Tevi complained.

"*Sybaline and I* are going. We need you here, looking after the gristmill. Besides, Sybaline fell into the streambed yesterday, and she took our wheelbarrow with her. All of our supplies fell out and are still there. We need them picked up."

Tevi pouted, but Marlys looked happy enough to have a task to accomplish.

Sybaline and Nettle gathered what they'd need for the journey into town, which mainly consisted of two lanterns and a shawl for each of them that they'd found in the gristmill. Without the sun above, the world was the same temperature as a cool fall night.

Facing the direction of town, Sybaline told herself she'd made this walk a thousand times before. She'd always been the one to run Momma's letters to the post office, and she'd usually picked up Momma's seed orders at the supply store. Telling herself this, though, didn't make it any less true that the walk now would be very different than any walk before.

Beside her, Nettle took a breath and held out her lantern. Sybaline did the same, keeping her booted feet in the shadows of her skirts. She wiggled her numb toes inside the leather, not willing to take them off lest they get even more unnaturally cold. Against her back, Nettle's hair hung in lazy clumps, not pulled into braids for the first time that Sybaline could remember. It made shadows stretch across the shoulders of her dress, the long winding ropes of vines hanging down the trunk of a tree.

CHAPTER 18

In relief, Sybaline and Nettle found that the path to town was much easier to walk than the one that led to Nettle's house. Sybaline hadn't raised any random walls of water between the gristmill and town. This meant they were able to walk along the gravel road that led directly to Main Street.

The road they walked followed the valley floor and the meandering path the river used to take. That flowing water had long been a source of both livelihood and terror for her family. It had flooded often enough in the past that they knew to watch the rhythms of its currents as they churned during the rainy season.

Now, though, they had no river. The edge of their bubble stared back at them—a wall of depthless black that reflected the light of their lanterns and gobbled up the shadows of their bodies. The hungry water beside them seemed to watch their progress, and Sybaline touched the magic that held the barrier at bay, making sure it was solid and firm and holding strong. Then, she pressed her hand against the wall itself. The temperature felt less like that of sun-warmed grass midsummer and more like that of melting snow puddling in cupped hands.

Shivering, she drew away. It was as if the chill snuck into her bones, though, because her cold toes tingled and the muscles in her calves cramped. She tried to shake out her feet as she walked, but that only caused her to stumble.

It was as they were almost into town that they passed a hollowed-out tree in the road. Sybaline came to a stop, staring at the tree and at the intersection it marked. This small road used to lead to—

"The Rothfords' house is that way," she said, her words taking a moment to unstick from her throat. Her bubble hadn't saved the Rothfords' house. Sybaline didn't know if the Rothfords refused to move or if they'd given up and left for the city. "Had I made the barrier stretch that way, I could have saved them."

"It's not your fault if they stayed," Nettle said.

"It's not *not* my fault," Sybaline said back.

Nettle lifted her lantern high and held it close to the wall of water. She turned her face and pressed her ear to the darkness.

Sybaline held her breath, though she didn't know for what. The only thing that would be swimming on the other side were fish, not the Rothfords, and if the Rothfords hadn't moved, they were dead.

"Sometimes, people die," Nettle said. She stood a beat longer, looking into the water that had swallowed whole the houses and lives of their neighbors, then turned away from the barrier and continued down the road.

They reached town without quite knowing they'd reached town. The gravel road here was dry, not soaked through with the same layer of dampness that had pooled in Auntie Wooline's garden. Stillness surrounded them, the shadowy memory of bustling townsfolk overlapping the quiet and unmoving street. Buildings rose in the darkness, their lantern light not able to reach both sides of the street at once. The world beyond watched them, the unblinking eyes of fish swimming just above the rooftops.

"Henderson's Grocery," Nettle whispered, pointing to one side of the street.

"And Barty's Barbershop," Sybaline whispered back, pointing in the other direction.

They walked down Main Street, naming the places they'd grown up knowing. The knit shop where their mommas used to buy yarn and bolts of cloth to make clothes. The post office where they learned all the news of the world and got letters from Poppa. The supply store where they bought jars for canning food. Until finally, they stood in the middle of the street with two small pools of light shining over their feet and the immense darkness stretching beyond and the metal movie theater sign hovering somewhere above where they couldn't see.

"Holy mackerel!" Nettle shouted, making Sybaline jump. She punched both fists in the air. "If we can make the electricity work in town, we can watch all the movies we want!"

"They probably didn't leave the movie film or equipment behind. Besides, making the electricity work here isn't like making the waterwheel at your house work. This has got to be more difficult than figuring out how to get water to run through the stream," Sybaline said.

"You don't know that. It's not like we don't have plenty of time to try to figure it out anyway." She crooked her head at Sybaline, then said in a low creepy voice. "We have *all the time in the world*."

Sybaline shoved her cousin away and walked to the front doors of the theater. Objects beyond the window reflected her light when she held it close. Gripping the curved door handle, she pulled on it but found it bolted fast.

"The door's locked. Why would they lock the door?" she asked.

"They probably didn't want looters getting in," Nettle said. "Or, you know…catfish burglars."

Sybaline stared at Nettle, her cousin's terrible joke sinking in.

"I sure thought something was fishy about these doors."

Sybaline dropped her head.

"What do you think the catfish burglars will do if they can't get inside? Scale the walls?"

Sybaline thumped her forehead against the glass door. Sound clattered inside the theater. She heard it, distant and muffled, as if whatever fell landed on something soft. She held a hand up to Nettle.

"Oh no," Nettle said. "I'm just getting started with these jokes—"

"*Shh.*" Sybaline pressed her ear flush against the glass. She closed her eyes and listened hard.

"What, are the fish already inside?"

The hair along the back of Sybaline's neck rose, prickling in the same way it had when long ago, she'd stood at the edge of a cliff with Poppa and heard a cougar scream.

"Sybaline?"

"Something's inside. I heard it." She cupped her hands around her eyes and tried to peer inside, but of course, the lights weren't on and her line of sight didn't extend far.

"I'll go around to the back of the building," said Nettle, low and quiet, not questioning what Sybaline had said. But then: "I'll bring a net, just in case we need to stop the catfish burglars," and then she disappeared, along with her lantern light, leaving Sybaline alone.

Sybaline left her lantern where it was beside the front door, hoping to use it as a distraction. If something was inside, it might focus on the pool of light and not track where Sybaline actually walked. Stepping away from the light drew her muscles tight. *You know where it is*, she said on repeat in her mind as her feet took her into the dark. Keeping one hand on the wall, her fingers scraped along brick and then smoothed over glass. They felt for the crease of the windows, searching for one that might be unlatched. *There.* A finger's wedge of space existed beneath a window that wasn't closed tight.

Grabbing hard, she slid open the window, even though fear churned in her belly. Whatever was inside wasn't a some*thing* but a some*one*. No animal knew how to use a window. A raccoon might, but it sure wouldn't close the window back behind it.

She asked herself who else might be stuck beneath the lake as she lifted one leg over the lip of the window and entered the pitch dark of the lobby inside the theater.

Her foot landed harder than she wanted, the step echoing through the lobby—if only it hadn't been so numb she might've been quieter—and the inside of the theater drew even more silent. It held its breath, an inhalation that, when broken, felt as if it would rush over her in a wave.

She reached for the magic, for its protection, but stopped

herself in time. She wouldn't allow herself to stop it from holding up the bubble.

Sound burst around her. Sudden light flooded from behind and threw her shadow across the burgundy-carpeted floor. She spun and made herself look big, like Poppa had taught her when she'd learned how to scare away animals, and she screamed.

CHAPTER 19

"*Ahh!*" A figure ran toward her, brandishing a long weapon. A light beam spun into the darkness—a flashlight!

"Stop!" Sybaline shouted. She used the same sort of tone Momma used when Sybaline tested her patience.

The person stopped, their upraised arm frozen in the air with the end of the flashlight shining directly in Sybaline's face.

Sybaline's heart beat too fast, but she kept her body still and controlled as she tried to peer around the light and see who stood before her.

"Sybaline?" said a boy, voice croaky and shaken.

"Do I know you?" Sybaline lifted an arm and blocked out the light, right as the boy dropped his own and let the end of the flashlight point at his face. His eyes blinked wide in the light. "*Fisch?* What are *you* doing here?"

"I'm not here on purpose." He collapsed in a heap, dropping the flashlight as he did. It rolled across the floor, and Sybaline scrambled after it before it could disappear.

When she turned around and shone the light back on him, she saw that it truly was Herbert Fisch, though he wasn't the Fisch she'd met weeks ago with his starched clothes and slicked-down hair.

"You look like you got in a fight with a bear," she said and sat beside him, patting him on the back when he began to sob.

Nettle found them some time later, sitting side by side in the dark, with the flashlight turned off to conserve battery. She had an open can of beans clasped in one hand and her lantern held in the other.

"You're eating my food supply!" Fisch cried, just as Sybaline said, "Where *were* you?"

"I found food," Nettle said, "and you found the *Fisch* burglar! Look how productive we both were."

"Did you *not* believe me that I heard something inside?" Sybaline asked.

"Oh, I believed you, but I also believed that I was hungry, and I was curious if any food had been left at the supply store."

"There's food there, but not a lot, and now you've eaten some of it," Fisch moaned. "If I ration it, it'll only last thirty-two more days. I'll starve after that. Now that you two are here and eating my food, it'll be even shorter. Thirty-two divided by three is ten point six six six six six six forever sixes. That's not even two weeks. We'll be dead in two weeks."

"Yeah, only that's not true, because we know how to grow food," Nettle said between bites of beans.

"The sun's disappeared. How do you grow food without sunlight?" Fisch asked, brows rising.

Nettle waved away the question. "We learned how to find food in the dark a long time ago."

"And we know how to catch fish," Sybaline said.

"We're not helpless."

Fisch tensed beside Sybaline. "I'm not helpless."

"I wasn't saying you were," Sybaline said, at the same time Nettle said, "You sure seem like it."

"I've lived here for weeks by myself!" He stood, hands clenched beside his thighs. He shivered, despite the coat he wore. "I've survived all by my lonesome. No one's been here to help me."

"Calm down, Fischy. You're right. You're not helpless. You've done a very good job surviving." Nettle settled herself beside Sybaline, with her back pressed against the wall.

"Why are you here?" Sybaline asked Fisch. "You shouldn't be in town at all—why didn't you leave before the waters rose?"

"You think I didn't try? I *tried*." Fisch loomed before them, the light from Nettle's lantern making him grow an extra three feet. "I have a tradition that I do before my family moves from one dam site to the next. I like to go down and watch the water rise. Usually, I watch at the bottom of the dam where my dad says it's safe, but this time, I decided walk farther out and see your valley. I just…I wanted to see it for myself. I went to your town because I knew it wouldn't flood first. It's higher in elevation than other places, so I thought it wouldn't go underwater for days and days. From town, I walked to the flooding bank of the big river and watched the water creeping up higher. I only explored for half a day; I camped in the theater at night, and then in the morning I decided to head home. But you won't believe what happened. I went to leave, except…" Fisch sucked in a deep breath, and Sybaline and Nettle exchanged a glance, knowing exactly how his story was about to end. "A *wall of water* had risen in the air."

Fisch raised his arms at the same time he said *wall of water*. The drama of it shone over his face. He stayed like that for a moment, but after a silent pause, he glanced at Sybaline and Nettle and then his arms flopped to his sides.

"You don't believe me," he said.

"Oh, we believe you," Nettle said.

"We were here too," Sybaline added. "We've seen the wall."

"Oh." Fisch flushed. He shoved his hands into his pockets. His disheveled hair cast spiked shadows across the ceiling. "I guess I've spent the past weeks trying to figure out how I'd tell somebody what happened here. I guess I was excited to tell you."

"You can still tell us," Sybaline said, trying to be nice.

"It was a *wa-wall of wat-water.*" The words broke as they came out of Fisch, his voice cracking.

"Yeah." Nettle pointed her thumb at Sybaline. "That was her fault. We hadn't meant to save the town... If she hadn't pushed out our wall of water, you would've had time to escape."

"It wasn't my fault," Sybaline said.

Nettle looked at Sybaline, aghast. "Whose fault then do you think it was?"

"The government!" Sybaline smacked one fist into her opposite open palm.

"You're being dramatic, Syb."

"It's true! The government destroyed our lives and ripped away our land and made it so my poppa doesn't have a home to come home to."

"You can't blame your choices on someone else," Nettle said.

"The government isn't actually a person," Fisch pointed out.

Sybaline slouched against the wall, scooting down to hide her face against her knees. She said again, "It wasn't my fault," even though she knew it was. *Everyone* was here because of her.

The ache of it burned in her chest right between each of her rib bones; it hurt in a way that made it difficult to breathe.

Nettle patted Sybaline's knees, though Sybaline didn't quite feel the pat-pat motion. The tingling numbness of her feet had crept up her calves and into her joints. She reached down and scratched at the itchy, aching skin above her boots.

"If I might ask," Fisch said, crouching before them. "How exactly does someone make a wall of water? Because I've been trying to figure it out, and I can't think of a single scientific principle that would explain what happened."

"We have magic," Nettle said, still patting Sybaline's knee.

"Oh," Fisch said, as if that made all the sense in the world.

———

Fisch asked ten thousand questions about the magic while they packed all the things he'd managed to collect over the last weeks of exploring town, including a big ole pot that Nettle wanted.

Where does the magic live? In the earth.

Will the lake turn magic? Maybe.

What does the magic do? It helps the land to grow and prosper.

If magic can be used to grow things, can it be used to destroy things too? No!

How do you make it work? Ummm. With your...hands and...mind?

If you get really angry, is it more difficult to control? Yes and no. Mostly, yes.

Are you superheroes? No (said Sybaline). Yes (said Nettle).

Can we use magic to escape? We've tried. It doesn't seem possible.

Why didn't your family use magic to stay along with you? Or use magic to stop the dam? It wasn't worth the risk, Nettle said, after waiting a long, *long* pause for Sybaline to answer.

"I suppose you've saved us from having to explore and gather supplies on our own," Nettle said a bit glumly, as she folded the thick blanket Fisch had been sleeping on.

"I scoured all of Main Street," Fisch said, perking up at having been complimented by Nettle, though he didn't seem to hear her very sad tone of voice. "I searched all the businesses for tools that could be useful and all the food I could find."

"You didn't go off Main Street?" Sybaline asked.

"No way. Would *you* have explored all the darkness? There could be holes a person could get lost inside!"

"You had a flashlight."

"A flashlight with batteries that will probably die soon. Think how bad it'd be to die in the dark of the movie theater but think how much *worse* it'd be to die out in the dark with the water rising everywhere."

Nettle snorted and continued filling a wooden sled Fisch had found in a closet. When it was full, they picked up the ropes and dragged it down the road, heading back to Nettle's house. When Fisch heard there was a possibility they could make the electricity at Nettle's house work, he'd whooped.

They walked along the road, boots crunching over the gravel with the sled scraping the ground behind them.

"Have you ever looked into the dark?" Fisch asked.

"And had the dark look back?" Nettle said in her creepy voice.

"What? No. Watch this." Fisch pulled his flashlight from his pocket and flipped it on. Stepping close to the barrier, he pressed the glass of the light against the water. The beam speared the darkness, brightening the black to a dark green.

Bits of muck and grime floated in the water, clouds of sediment turning the liquid foggy and thick, almost exactly like the exhalations of the Smoky Mountains on dim mornings when mist clung to treetops and blanketed the valley in a quilt of condensed breath. On mornings such as those, with the sun brightening water droplets in the air, Sybaline felt hope. Now, all she felt was dread, and it darkened the edges of her vision and crawled goose bumps over her arms.

"What if we saw a person floating by?" Nettle whispered.

Sybaline shoved away from the barrier and the sudden terrible image of the Rothfords. "Why do you have to say things like that?"

"I say the things I think." Nettle grabbed the flashlight from Fisch and pressed her nose to the edge of water. "It's a curse."

"You saying the things you think is a curse on all of us!" Sybaline's temper rose as she watched the lake. Inside the darkness had once been peoples' homes. "Leaving a place you love is a terrible thing."

"I've never loved a place so much that it was hard to leave," Fisch said, quiet.

Sybaline struggled to find a way to explain a truth to which belonged no words. Blinking hard, she picked up the sled ropes she'd dropped and leaned her weight into them. But only when her two companions joined her did it move down the road.

CHAPTER 20

The walk back to Nettle's took longer than the walk to town. Sybaline braced herself, hoping the strange layer of water that had filled Auntie Wooline's garden would be disappeared by the time they made it to the gristmill, but sure enough, as they dropped into the deepest part of the valley the Larks called home, glistening mud shone against the grass.

"Where's it coming from?" Sybaline asked.

"The ground's too saturated." Fisch knelt, his flashlight aimed at the ground. "The lake water's pressing down around us and the earth is soaking it right up. The water's got to have someplace to go, so it's going *here*."

"When will it go somewhere else?" Nettle asked.

Fisch looked up, a deep crease forming between his brows. "It probably won't. If anything, it'll just get deeper."

The three stood where they were, none of them seeming to know quite what to do. Eventually, Sybaline walked through the mud, tugging the sled behind her, and headed onto the porch of the gristmill. She couldn't solve the problem of the saturated ground, but she could try to solve the problem of the gristmill's electricity.

"Marlys! *Tevi!*" Nettle shouted.

After a pause, thundering footsteps echoed through the dark. The two small girls whooped as they hurtled down the empty stream.

When she reached them, Tevi bent in half, heaving in gasps of air. "If you don't think about maybe tripping, you can run real fast down the stream."

"There aren't any trees to run into in there." Marlys climbed up and over the bank. "What are *you* doing here?" she asked Fisch.

"What are *you* doing here?" he asked in response.

"This is my home." With her fists set on her hips, she looked just like all the aunties of their family, fierce and scary when they needed to be.

Fisch's shoulders slumped. "I can't get to my home."

Marlys's hands fell to her sides, arms hanging limp. "Oh," was all she said.

Together, they all sat on the porch, with the supplies from town in front of them on the sled and the supplies from Sybaline's house piled behind them. Marlys and Tevi had carried them in but had done little to no organizing.

Restlessness shifted inside Sybaline. She strained to peer through the darkness surrounding the gristmill. The only points of light were the fire they'd allowed to die down to burning coals and the two lanterns they'd lit and placed on either side of the porch.

To their left ran the hollow outline of the streambed they needed to fill with water. The problem was the creek in front of Sybaline's house. They hadn't thought to keep water in the stream.

"Could we tear a small hole in the bubble?" Sybaline asked, not liking the thought even as she said it.

"Like when you tried to tear down the wall you built in front of Tevi, and it looked like the entire bubble was about to collapse?" Nettle said. "No. Bad idea."

"I'd rather not have the bubble collapse," Fisch said.

"Me neither," Tevi echoed.

"We'd suffocate and drown," Fisch said. "Though drowning is supposed to be a very peaceful way to die."

Both Sybaline and Nettle turned, mouths agape, to face Fisch.

"What? I read a news article once about it," Fisch said. "It was a guy who'd drowned but hadn't actually died. Later when he woke up in the hospital, he said drowning had been a very peaceful experience."

Sybaline and Nettle continued staring at Fisch.

"Drowning being peaceful doesn't mean I want to *try* it! All I'm saying is that it's better than dying of a lightning strike or falling off a cliff or getting crushed by rocks."

"Herbert," Nettle said. "You need to stop talking now."

"I worry about things, is all." Fisch huffed out a breath. He tapped his fingers together, then held one in the air. "If I'm allowed to speak, I might have an idea."

"We're listening," Nettle said, "as long as it doesn't have to do with drowning."

"You mentioned there's a creek that runs by your house. Why can't that water come to this stream?"

"That creek and this stream don't connect," Nettle said.

"Force the water to come this way. You can make a new path for it to travel along," Fisch said.

"Herb, you're brilliant!" Nettle said.

"We'd have to use magic," Sybaline said. The only times they'd used magic since living inside the bubble was when they needed to—when they thought they were being chased by a bear and when they needed to carve a path through the woods. This was different. Choosing to divert the natural path of a creek seemed very unnatural to Sybaline.

"I'll do it," Marlys said. "I'll use the magic and make the creek water come over here."

"No," Sybaline said, forcefully. "You aren't risking yourself.

This isn't a good use of magic. It's already bad enough that you're here." She reached over and squeezed Marlys's hand, trying to soften her words. "I'd be terrified for you to work the magic; I'm scared enough at the thought of doing it myself."

"Sometimes, being scared makes it seem like you can't do things," Fisch said.

"I'm better at being angry than being scared," Sybaline said. She'd been plenty angry before. Angry at the whole wide world. At the government. At Benjamin and Cedric and Momma. The only time she'd been scared was when she thought the water wall would collapse and when she thought a bear was going to eat them. Both times, she'd been sloppy with her magic.

"I'm scared plenty," Nettle murmured.

Sybaline turned toward her. "But you're the strongest person I know. You're not scared of anything!" She couldn't remember a single moment in her life that she'd known Nettle to be scared.

"I'm scared all the time. I was scared to stay here. I was scared not go to with my momma. I was scared to leave my baby sisters. I was scared to say goodbye to my family, not knowing if I'd ever see them again and not being able to tell them I was *actually* saying goodbye. I'm scared to work magic that feels unnatural and *wrong*. I'm scared, but being scared doesn't mean I can't also be brave."

Nettle's gaze stayed locked on Sybaline, none of the fear she spoke of lining her face. How was it possible her cousin had been so scared and Sybaline hadn't known it?

The word *brave* echoed inside the confines of Sybaline's thinking space. Weeks ago, she would've thought herself brave for deciding to stay in the valley and to fight for her home, but with the weight of the lake hanging over her, she wondered if it had been fear more than bravery that had motivated her choice.

Do you remember the fire? Benjamin had asked, rising up the image of Aunt Ethel standing before the wildfire, a wall of flames towering before her. She'd known exactly the risk she was taking when she used magic to save them; she'd known and she'd done it anyway.

Sometimes a person doesn't know quite what they're afraid of, Momma had said.

Do you know what you're afraid of? Sybaline had asked.

I've always known, Momma had said, shadows from firelight shifting over her face.

What was Sybaline afraid of? Worse, what had her fear made her do? Her fear had trapped Nettle and Marlys and Tevi and Fisch beneath the lake with her. It was her fault, and she had to make it right. She had to find a way for everyone to survive, no matter the risk.

I can be brave. Tenderly, she tested the fear that expanded in her chest, moth wings brushing against her ribs and trying to flutter free of her body.

I can be brave. She reached for the magic and for the creek beside her home, and she *pulled.*

The magic came to her. Its warmth filled her from the tips of her toes to the top of her head and every inch of space in between. It didn't comfort her as it once had. It *couldn't* bring comfort, because Sybaline now understood how dangerous the world was, with or without it. Having the magic truly didn't make life easier or better. It was just a thing she could decide to use or not use. And right now, she needed to use it.

She drew water from the creek that ran past Sybaline's house and used it to carve a path in the earth straight to the riverbed beside Nettle's gristmill. Once the process started, the water took over. Liquid flowed toward them, lapping at the rocks and stones of the streambed and returning sound to the dampened world.

The valley had been transformed into a place of silence and stale air. Now, trickles of water surrounded them, and relief at the normal, *so* normal noise weighed down her limbs, dragged her toward the earth. Beneath the bubble, her valley had changed exactly as she had, when the truth was, she hadn't wanted to change at all. She lived now beneath a grave mounded over by water. Her home had turned into a tomb, and she'd buried herself inside it.

Sybaline cried.

Tevi wrapped her arms around her, but otherwise, everyone ignored her, which was for the best. She'd never liked people watching as she broke. She preferred to do that in private, but privacy wasn't an option in the darkness beneath the lake.

Water rushed forward and met Nettle's house. The water-wheel creaked and began to spin. Power rolled through wires and into mechanisms Sybaline didn't understand. Until all at once, Nettle jumped to her feet and ran to the front porch, where she threw a switch.

Sudden, blinding light illuminated the yard. Hope shot through Sybaline, even as she ducked her head against her lap, sunspots forming blobby shapes in her vision. Beside her, Fisch cried out. Gingerly, she looked up, blinking and blinking and rubbing her watering eyes.

Each browning blade of grass was highlighted with light on one side and shadows on the other. The tree Auntie Wooline had decorated with lanterns stood crooked and proud, one stray lantern still dangling from a limb. Crystalline water flowed through the stream and danced with bubbles.

Nettle whooped and launched off the steps and was quickly followed by Marlys and Tevi. They ran across the brightened yard, feet squishing against mud beneath the grass, and splashed into the stream. Water kicked up in waves and fell over the already wet yard.

Beside Sybaline, Fisch gasped, and she realized he was crying as well. They were both a mess together, with tears streaking unbidden down their chins. They watched Sybaline's cousins play in the water.

"Come *on!*" Nettle shouted.

That was all the encouragement Sybaline needed. She wiped off her face with the sleeve of her dress and stepped off the porch. Even though she knew the light surrounding them wasn't actually warm, it took the chill off her skin. She kicked off her boots, and hitching up her skirts, splashed into the water. Energy zipped down her spine and for the first time in days, she laughed. Joy fell out of her, bubbles cascading from her and frothing into the air, just like the water at her feet.

Fisch flew, almost tripping and upending her. She stumbled and looked up in time to see him fall face-first into the stream.

"I'm going fishing for Fisch!" Nettle hollered and grabbed Herbert by the armpits to pull him out of the water.

"I *am* Fisch, and I'm fishing!" Fisch hollered back, which was such an awful joke that Sybaline choked on the water she now drank from her hands.

She bent to the quickly filling stream and slurped up

another gulp of water. When she stood, she let it dribble out her mouth. It slipped over her tongue and between her teeth, running down her neck and soaking into her dress and seeping into the sad nooks and crannies that had cracked open in the past months. It filled her.

"Sybaline?" Nettle asked.

Water pooled in the palms of Sybaline's hands. It dipped into the creases between her fingers. It dampened her skin and wet the cuff of her shirtsleeves.

"*Sybaline.*"

Sybaline looked up.

Nettle stood frozen before her, her dark gaze locked somewhere near Sybaline's feet. No smile lingered on her face or laughter sprouted from her throat, skin pulling tight around her eyes and mouth.

Sudden, confusing fear shuddered through Sybaline's body, though not through her legs, for they were numb as they had been for days. She took a step back, then stumbled out of the river altogether. When she looked down to where Nettle's gaze remained, it was to find the sodden cloth of her dress sticking to her knees.

And below that, the unmistakable bark of trees, shaped exactly like her feet.

CHAPTER 21

"It could be worse," Nettle said.

"*How?*" Sybaline sat before the fireplace, patting her legs dry and running the pads of her fingers over her skin—*not* skin.

"You could be turning into nightshade."

"Or a loblolly pine cone," said Fisch.

"Or a turkey tail mushroom," said Marlys.

"Or a daisy!" shouted Tevi.

"Or a stinky ramp," said Nettle.

Sybaline picked up the boots she'd shucked off earlier and threw one at Nettle. Her cousin ducked, revealing Fisch, who stood behind her. Sybaline's fury turned on him, and she threw her other shoe at him. "A *loblolly pine cone*? What do you know about pine cones? Who are you to say anything about *any* of this? You shouldn't even be here!"

"I'm only here because you made me get stuck here," Fisch said.

Sybaline turned back to the fire, hunching so she curled over her legs.

"Did you just start transforming now, Syb?" Nettle asked.

Ducking her head, Sybaline covered her face with her hands, not wanting to admit that *no*, her transformation had likely begun days and weeks before, when her feet first began to numb. She'd been transforming from the inside out, bones shifting first, and then her skin. Had she not refused to pay attention, could she have stopped the process?

She sat up. "I think I knew, but what good was there in finding out for certain? It's not like there's a way to turn myself back."

Nettle frowned.

Fisch picked up a log from beside the fireplace and set it inside the hearth at an angle that would only snuff out the flames. Marlys got up from her makeshift cot and fixed the log using an iron poker. Sparks flew up the chimney.

"Every time I've used magic since deciding to stay in the valley, it was out of desperation," Sybaline said. "What else could I have done?"

"Nothing," Nettle said, then: "We could've moved and not stayed in the valley."

Shame coiled through Sybaline, filling up all the gaps inside her that had once been so certain of her decision to stay.

"Are you going to have to stop using magic like Aunt Ethel?" Tevi asked.

"If I don't, I'll turn full-magic and end up like Papaw," she said. Considering she didn't want to completely transform, it was her only choice. She'd live like Bo, with flowers growing out of his head, and Aunt Ethel, with vines covering her shoulders. She swallowed hard, thinking of what might happen to her cousins and Fisch if she went full-magic and disappeared altogether. "It was selfish of me to stay here."

"I don't know that you were selfish," Nettle said. "I think it's more that you were scared."

This again. *Fear*. And the fact that Sybaline hadn't understood how to be brave. That it would've been brave to leave the valley in the first place, even though it wasn't what she wanted.

Sybaline's voice felt thick, as if she had a cold and gunk coated her throat. She forced herself to say, "I didn't want to leave home, and I didn't want to change into someone new, so I stayed, and then I ended up changing anyway."

Nettle dragged her hands down her face, then she stood and headed toward the front door with a lantern in one hand. "No matter what's happening now, none of us are going to be able to think about it clearly. My momma always says you shouldn't make important decisions when you haven't slept enough. I'm going to go pick up extra wood from outside to get us through the night, and then the five of us are going to *sleep*. Come morning, we'll figure out what to do."

Sybaline drew back up the hem of her dress, so it revealed her feet and shins. Skin tangled with bark below her knee, the grains of wood curving over her shin and drawing soft lines down to her foot. Bending her toes, she winced, noticing how much range of motion she'd lost.

A spot outside her right ankle itched. She dug her nails against it, scratching the strange mottling of wood and skin. A smidgen of bark peeled away and from it unfurled a small, green leaf. Another came out as well, until a ring of green leaves encircled her entire ankle. She recognized the elongated shape of the leaf. *Laurel.* She was turning into a laurel plant with its thin, waxy leaves that drooped in winter. They encircled tree branches in a ladderlike pattern; bracelets stacked along an arm. There were ten thousand laurel trees filling her valley and *all* the valleys of the Smoky Mountains. How long would it take for her to become one of them?

She reached for her wool socks and drew them over her feet, stuffing the leaves inside to hide away the consequence of what she'd done.

"I thought staying would be worth it," she said. "I convinced myself that using the magic to save the valley meant I wouldn't transform. Benjamin was right all along: he said I was trying to save myself, that I wasn't really trying to save the valley at all."

Beside her, Fisch turned away from where he was laying blankets on the floor for himself to sleep and looked at her carefully, as if what she was saying mattered more than anything else. "Has staying and overusing the magic been worth it?"

"Yes…*no.* Maybe—I don't know." She dug her fingers into her hair. "How can I know the answer to that?"

"It can be worth it and not worth it at the same time. I punched Charlie Borg in the nose last summer when he wouldn't stop pulling on the back of my sister's dress. That was worth it and not worth it at the same time."

Sybaline's gaze skittered away from his face. She'd never thought to ask about his family, if he had sisters or brothers or how terribly much his family must miss him. Did they think he was dead?

She drew in a deep breath. "I was so mad at you when we first met. You talked about these mountains, about my *home* as if it were a plaything. Some toy or game you could use up."

"I didn't mean to sound like that."

"You didn't *mean* to, but you did. I was mad because I didn't know how to make you understand what this valley means to me. This place isn't a plaything at all. It's not a bauble. It's…" Sybaline closed her eyes and opened the palms of her hands, feeling the warmth of the magic as it made a bed of her skin to rest against. "It's life. It's old and calm. It makes me feel whole.

I know that sounds strange, but it's real and it's true. Without the valley, how can I still be whole?"

"You'd figure it out. People change all the time, and they change for the better, even if it's hard." Fisch settled himself beside her, his legs sticking out straight, as if he were the one being turned to wood instead of her. "I understand not liking change. I've moved so often, and every time is as hard as the last."

Sybaline eyed Fisch and found in his face the same worry lines that lived in Momma's skin, and maybe...maybe if she were to look in a mirror, she would find the same lines on hers. Maybe they all were carrying heavy burdens, and she'd been too focused on herself to notice.

She nodded. Fisch nodded back. They may not really understand one another fully, but they understood parts of each other, and for now, that was enough.

By the time Nettle returned with a fresh supply of logs to burn and small branches for kindling, Fisch and Sybaline had made a comfy bed of blankets for them to sleep on before the fire. Marlys and Tevi were already fast asleep in their sleeping places, having grown bored with the conversation. When Nettle turned off the lights in the gristmill, they all lay still, listening to the warm crackle of the fire.

"At least the darkness is a choice, now," Fisch said.

"Only in this house." Sybaline understood deeply that this life she'd made for herself wasn't much of a life at all, where the only place they had light and warmth was at the gristmill.

They slept, though at some point during the night, Sybaline found herself awake and watching the rise and fall of Nettle breathing, hurting with the thought of how she'd trapped her cousins in the dark and cold beside her. Nettle's hair spun out like spiderwebs of lace across the floor. Sybaline brushed it back and down so it wouldn't snarl in Nettle's sleep, but as she did, her fingers met with the threads of spindly roots.

Fingers moving slow, lest she wake Nettle, she picked up the hair that wasn't hair and held it against the flickering light of the fireplace. The white flesh of ginseng glowed in the light. It was the root of a plant Momma sometimes used as an herbal remedy. People paid good money for wild ginseng, though her family didn't believe in digging it up just to sell.

Sybaline wasn't the only one to have begun transforming. Nettle was too.

Sybaline had tried very hard to make of her life what she wanted, but instead, she'd separated herself from the living world and from her family. She'd taken what was most precious to her and twisted it, forced it to take on a new, unrecognizable shape. This valley had once been the core of her, but then she'd gone and changed both it and her. Whatever she was now, it wasn't what she'd been, and whatever the valley was now, it wasn't what it'd been before either.

She had to leave this place, and she had to figure out how to take her family, and Fisch, with her.

Sybaline set the tender roots of the ginseng plant back on the floor. She tucked her hand beneath the blanket covers, palm cupping her cheek, then curled her knees to her chest. And there she stayed, still as she could, while silent tears fell.

CHAPTER 22

Light blazed. Sybaline tossed up her hands to block out the brightness, but as soon as her hands left the warmth beneath her blanket, she squealed and tucked them back under. She peeked open her eyes, squinting against the bright light from where someone had turned on the electricity. Cool ash filled the fireplace with only a few burning coals still left inside, a shade of orange that said they needed to be used now to light a new fire lest they go out altogether.

The night before, Nettle had slept between Sybaline and her two sisters on her opposite side, but now, that space was empty. Sybaline turned over beneath her covers to find a body-shaped blob on her other side—Fisch huddled beneath his own blankets. Behind him, condensation rimmed the window, and beyond that, the darkness of the lake pressed against the glass.

"It's so cold," Sybaline said.

"It's been getting colder every day since the water closed overhead," Fisch mumbled from beneath his blankets, his head tucked completely under. "We're probably going to die from hypothermia. It's either that or starvation."

Sybaline poked the place where Fisch's forehead should be.

"*Ouch.*" He pulled down the edge of the blankets and glared at her.

"You have dark thoughts, Fisch."

"Realistic thoughts."

"I've never thought about dying."

He pulled down the blanket farther. "I have! I've known it would get colder, possibly too cold to live, and I knew at some point I would run out of food. Those were my two big worries… beyond the bubble collapsing."

Nettle walked across the room and added kindling to the barely burning coals in the hearth. "The fire went out earlier, and none of us bothered to wake up to add more logs."

"I thought about it," Fisch said, "but I was too cold to get up."

"You're going to have to get over that," Nettle said. "How are we supposed to get anything done if we refuse to work when it's cold?"

"It feels like winter," Tevi said from a corner of the room. She stood by the pile of stray clothes and blankets they'd dumped in one corner and was trying to find the neck hole in a shirt. Her arms stuck through the sleeves and her head disappeared somewhere inside.

Beside her, Marlys tied an apron around her shoulders like a shawl, and then reached over to help her sister pull her head through her shirt.

"It feels like winter, and we can compare it to the winter, but only if we remember that this winter will *never end*," Fisch said.

Sybaline's heart sunk. He was right. There would never be a time when the earth would tilt, sliding them closer to the sun, and her home would heat. The valley would always be buried beneath hundreds of feet of cold, dark water.

With a rush, she threw off her covers and stumbled to where her boots were set to the right of the fireplace. She shoved her feet into them, only glancing briefly at her legs and the place where the bark of her skin stretched above her sock and had begun creeping over her knees. She'd already lost movement in her ankles and toes. How bad would things become if—*when*—her knees stopped working as well? How could she live as half a tree? This wasn't at all like Bo with the flowers on his head.

"Humidity is rising," Fisch said from where he now stood with his nose pressed to the window. "I hadn't considered this part. Interesting."

"*How?*" came Nettle's reply, the word falling out of her on a shuddering breath.

Sybaline turned from the fire at the scared sound of her cousin's voice. Nettle stuck her nose to the window as well, leaning close to Fisch.

"*How* is that happening?" Nettle asked. "Fog shouldn't be able to exist down here."

Sybaline climbed to her feet and squeezed between the pair. The lights to Nettle's front porch illuminated the yard in a perfect circle, curving against the darkness and lighting the place where drops of dew clung to the grass. All throughout the front yard, where the silky sheen of water glistened among the grass and where the water funneled down the streambed, wisps of smoke rose in curling waves.

"The water down here doesn't have anywhere to go, no sky for the clouds to float into," Fisch said. "They're staying on the ground."

The fog seeped into the air above the water, thin streams of ghosts rising into the sky. Sybaline asked, "This is bad, isn't it?"

"It certainly isn't good." Fisch stepped away from the window and went to the pile of clothes Marlys and Tevi had already scoured. He dragged out extra clothes and layered them over what he already wore. "That fog is made up of water droplets. When we walk through it, we'll get wet, and the wetter we are, the colder we'll feel."

Sybaline followed after Fisch and began digging through

the pile of supplies to see what other clothes she could wear. When she came up empty, she sat back, feet flat on the ground, crouching over her knees.

They had no other clothes at Nettle's or at her own house. That meant they would have to travel back into town sooner rather than later to see what else they could find. How much colder would it get? Would they need to find true winter clothing? What kind of weather systems did a *bubble* have? Would the fog keep rising? Would temperatures keep going down? Would it start frosting out? Would it *snow*?

Sybaline pushed against her knees and stood, not wanting to ask out loud if it were possible for it to snow. Fisch would probably say yes.

Fisch opened the front door, and Marlys and Tevi ran outside. Marlys whooped as she ran through the fog, swirls of mist trailing about her legs. Nettle turned to follow, but Sybaline grabbed her arm. Her cousin spun, the spindles of her hair flying out and catching the light.

"Did you know this was happening?" Sybaline took hold of one of the bits of roots and dragged it around so it rested against Nettle's nose, forcing her to look at it cross-eyed. "Did you know you were transforming?"

"It would've been hard not to notice, seeing as how the roots are connected to my head," Nettle said, brows lifted, as if to say, *how did you* not *notice your legs changing?* She pulled away from Sybaline's grasp.

They stood, an arm's length of cold air and dewy distance between them. Guilt tugged hard at Sybaline. It roosted somewhere inside the tissue of her lungs, talons burying deep.

Sybaline started to reach up to Nettle's hair again, but dropped her hand when Nettle took a step back. "Why didn't you tell me?"

"What would have been the point?" Nettle raised her arms in the air and made hooks of her hands, as if trying to grab at the whole of the upside-down glass giant's bowl. "I've been here with you the whole time. We've worked the same magic. If you were transforming, then obviously I probably was too. It's just like you said: it's not like we could do anything about it. There are risks to every decision we make. That's been our whole lives, though, Syb. We've always been making choices, taking risks, and hoping things turn out okay. That's what I did. I took a risk. I made a choice. *I* used the magic wrong, and I'll keep doing it if that's what I decide. The magic and the valley might be the most important thing to you, but my family is the most important thing to me. *You're* the most important thing to me." A sad smile turned up the edges of Nettle's mouth. "You're just like my sisters; I'd do anything for you."

CHAPTER 23

"The only way to escape the bubble is by using magic," Sybaline said to the empty house. Everyone stood in the yard, picking through the supplies they'd left in Fisch's sled, acting as if the entire world hadn't shifted.

"I wish we had a teakettle," Nettle said, her voice drifting in from outside.

"I wish we had mittens," Marlys said, her voice following her sister's.

Sybaline stuffed her own cold hands beneath her armpits. She stepped onto the porch and then crossed to the place where the light grew dim and couldn't push through the darkness. She peered through it, wondering how she could twist it and make escape possible.

"You have scary eyes," Tevi said.

Sybaline jerked around and found her littlest cousin standing beside her, a long scarf wrapped over her ears. Taking up one end of the scarf, Sybaline tucked it beneath Tevi's collar so it wouldn't come undone. She said, "You're a snowman."

"Except I'm not made of snow."

"No." Sybaline patted the top of the scarf, pushing it flat so it cocooned Tevi's ears. "No, you aren't."

Tevi pressed forward and rubbed her forehead against Sybaline's collarbone, making Sybaline laugh.

"First priority for the day should be getting more firewood," Sybaline said, thinking of how cold Tevi was, not that Tevi would ever complain about it.

"I don't know how get firewood," Fisch said.

"First priority should be gathering food," Nettle corrected. "That can of beans I ate feels like a year ago."

"I don't know how to gather food either," Fisch said.

"You get food, and I get wood?" Sybaline said to Nettle, who nodded. Sybaline would have to try and think of ways to escape the bubble while she was out chopping wood.

Nettle headed back into the house and came out again with two lanterns, both lit. One, she handed to Sybaline and Tevi. The other, she kept for herself and Marlys.

"What do I do?" Fisch asked.

"Umm," Nettle said.

Truth be told, Sybaline didn't know Fisch well enough to know how he could help. He'd done a good job of surviving this long, but he'd done so in town when he'd been able to scavenge. Did he know how to scavenge in the forest or how to pick food from Nettle's momma's garden? Did he even know what food looked like when it wasn't set out on a nice plate by his own mother?

"I'm supposed to sit here and wait for you all to come back?" Fisch asked.

Sybaline said, "You can try to come up with a way to keep the house warm. Maybe we can extra insulate it or something."

"You're telling me to sit here and think." Fisch crossed to the porch and sat, taking up the unlit lantern off the top step and clutched it to his chest. "That's all I've been doing for weeks now. Sitting around and thinking of ways to solve problems I don't know how to solve."

"Then you're probably really good at it." Nettle turned and walked around the house where the garden grew. Marlys trailed after, carrying an empty basket.

Fisch huffed out a cranky breath.

Sybaline gathered the wheelbarrow and axe they'd brought from her house, while Tevi took up the lantern, holding it carefully before of her. They crossed to the edge of the forest and began scouring for a fallen tree they could chop into smaller pieces.

It didn't take long for Sybaline to sweat while chopping wood. It trickled down her spine and ringed her neck. Fear bedded beneath the moisture, because she knew it was just like what Fisch said about the fog. If she was wet, it would make her feel more cold. A shudder worked through her, and she began making plans of how to dry off before finding clean clothes to wear and airing out her clothes before the fire.

All while she worked, she attempted to make plans for how to escape, though she didn't come up with anything that didn't require the use of magic.

When she and Tevi arrived back at the mill, pushing the full wheelbarrow, it was to find Nettle standing on the porch, her hair pulled back in a messy bun that was caked with dirt. Marlys sat on the porch, peeling ears of corn.

"Did he go with you?" Nettle asked.

"Who?" Sybaline asked.

"*Who?* Who else is here that I'd ask about?"

"Fisch disappeared," Marlys said.

Sybaline glanced around the porch, as if Fisch were about to jump out from around the corner. "He's not inside?"

Marlys tossed down the corn. "He's not inside or around the back or anywhere. We looked. He didn't respond when Nettle shouted for him."

The shiver that started in Sybaline's skin earlier increased; this time, layering into the meat of her core. "Why would he leave?"

Nettle stared right back at Sybaline, answerless.

"This is bad," Sybaline whispered, for she didn't trust Fisch's navigation skills when the sun shone, much less when it was pitch black out.

"Bless him," Nettle muttered. "With all that talk about death, he might have gone and gotten himself killed."

Worried, Sybaline hunkered close to the ground with the lantern shedding light on the grass and mud. Blades were broken off and smashed by their feet but others stood tall. She tried to pick out which set of prints might belong to Fisch.

Beside her, Nettle walked toward the place where light met darkness and placed two fingers between her lips. A sharp whistle erupted from her mouth. Their family had long used sharp whistles to call to one another across distances. A whistle might not bend around the curves and knolls of the mountains, but it pierced through other sounds, like the rush of river water and the rustle of tree leaves.

"Fisch doesn't know the signal," Sybaline said, returning to examine the grass, trying to pick out Fisch's footprints from among all the prints they'd made that morning.

"He might not know what the whistles mean, but he's more likely to hear that than our shouts." Nettle whistled again, then cupped her hands over her mouth and yelled, "Fisch! *Fisch!*"

Sybaline listened. Unbroken but for the sound of the stream, silence surrounded them.

"I can use magic to find him," Tevi said from where she was hunkered down, peering at the grass, too.

"No!" both Sybaline and Nettle shouted.

"I'll use just a little magic," she said. "Not enough to turn into a pigweed or anything."

Nettle bent down and cupped Tevi's small, scarf-wrapped head between her hands. "You aren't using magic for *anything*. If anyone's taking the risk, it's the grown-ups."

"You're not grown-ups."

"We're closer to grown than you," Sybaline said. Her heart had fallen into her belly at the thought of Tevi working magic and transforming. It now beat a frail rhythm.

"You two stay here and shuck corn and pile up the wood inside," Nettle said.

"We always get left behind!" Tevi stood tall, vibrating with anger. "You left us behind when you stayed here. You left us behind when you went to town and found Fisch. Now you're leaving us again."

"We're not leaving you behind," Sybaline said.

"Yes, you are! You're *leaving*!" Tevi's voice turned shrill, straining with tension Sybaline understood.

She bent, looking into the shadows of Tevi's face where

tear tracks drew red stripes down her cheeks. "I thought once that everyone left me too. Poppa and Cedric and Benjamin, even Momma. It hurt."

Tevi pinched her lips together, chin quivering and shoulders shaking.

Everyone left, Sybaline remembered thinking. She'd thought everyone was leaving the valley; she understood now that perhaps her entire fear was the same one as Tevi's. Not that her family was leaving their home, but that they were leaving *her*. She understood now that everyone had been busy living their own lives, and sometimes *living their own life* meant taking a path Sybaline wasn't traveling on. She thought Tevi might not understand that, though, so instead, all she said was, "What I want most in the whole entire world is for you to be safe. The gristmill is the safest place right now. Nettle and I will come back; we'll always come back."

Marlys came up behind Tevi and wrapped her in a big hug. Tevi leaned back against her sister, saying, "Promise?"

"I promise," Sybaline said, and then before she could change her mind, she took hold of her lantern and headed into the darkness, Nettle following close behind.

"We might have to use magic to find him," Nettle murmured when they were out of earshot of her sisters.

"I know," Sybaline said, grim.

They found Fisch's muddy footprints. Fisch's feet were bigger than any of theirs, and so while tracking him in the dark was difficult, it wasn't impossible. His path led in a swooping circle around the gristmill's property, cutting close to the woods and then back away again, until suddenly, it plunged straight between two trees and disappeared into the forest.

Nettle took them into the trees, leading the way, following until—

"That fool."

Sybaline pushed past Nettle and reached out, already knowing what she'd find; her fingers collided with a thin barrier of water, tall and impenetrable.

"We didn't think to warn him about the tunnels," Nettle said.

"Why would we have ever thought we'd need to?" She slid her hand along the wall she'd accidentally built and found the place where it opened. Fisch must've walked through there.

"I'll go in," Sybaline said. "If anyone's going to work magic, it should be me."

"It should be *me*," Nettle said. "You've transformed more than I have. Your feet are all tree! Only my hair is ginseng."

Thick emotions swirled through Sybaline. They turned

her tender and bruised; she would fall to pieces if Nettle were to push her in just the right place. "I should be the one to take all the risks."

Nettle hovered beside her, quiet and still. Then: "What?"

"You know what. And you know why. This is all because of me! You. Marlys and Tevi. Fisch."

"You didn't *make* me stay. I made that choice all by myself. Don't you dare take that away from me."

Frustrated, Sybaline paced backward, putting space between her and Nettle. "It's *my fault*."

"No, it isn't."

"It feels like it is."

"Sometimes feelings are wrong." Nettle closed the gap between them, reached out and took up her hand. "I made the choice, too, and that's my fault. You can't take on all the blame yourself."

Sybaline held tight to Nettle's hand, grounding herself in her cousin's strength. She'd always thought herself the rational, responsible one, but it turned out that wasn't quite the case. "We're going to find Fisch, then we're going to figure out how to escape this place. We can't live like this." She paused. She'd heard herself say the words, but it took a moment to realize she'd spoken them aloud. She'd only decided they needed to leave hours ago, but already, it felt like an eternity.

Squeezing Sybaline's hand three times in an *I love you,* Nettle said, "You're sure?"

"Whatever I thought staying here would be, I was wrong. This was my home—it *is* my home—but it's not where I need to be any longer. It's time to find home somewhere else."

CHAPTER 24

They realized Fisch was following the trail they'd carved in the woods between Sybaline's house and the gristmill. The trail itself had become difficult to follow, not because the plants had regrown, but because an inch of water had risen, turning the path into mud.

They came to a place where the wall opened up and then cut in several directions. Sybaline vaguely remembered this place, except Nettle had been the one to lead, and she'd known the direction they needed to head to find the gristmill. Here, Fisch's muddy prints stopped. He must've stepped off the trail and gone in a different direction.

"This is bad," Nettle said.

"Fisch!" Sybaline yelled.

Nettle whistled again, and—

"*Help!*" came a tinny response.

Sybaline whooped.

"Are you there?" Fisch called, his voice thready thin and

cracking. "Is it you? Did you find me? How do I get out? Get me out!"

"Dummy," Nettle said, though the relief on her face contrasted with her sharply muttered word.

"I got lost," Fisch shouted. The scratchiness of his voice told Sybaline he must've been yelling for a while.

"We don't know which way you walked! The wall branches in different directions, forming tunnels," Sybaline shouted back. "You're going to have to go back the way you came."

"How? I don't which way I walked either. It's all dark."

"Dark?" Nettle shouted. "Don't you have your lantern?"

Silence fell. It crawled into the holes of the tunnels and ate up what remained of the echoes of Fisch's voice.

"Fisch?" Nettled pressed her knuckles to her eye sockets. "What happened to your lantern?"

The quietest whimper reached them. He said, "I dro—ack... tunnel...out."

"Talk louder, Fisch," Nettle said.

"I dropped it, and the light went out! I'm in a maze." Fisch's voice grew quieter, clearly moving away through the rabbit-warren-like tunnels.

Sybaline's heartbeat ratcheted up. "Fisch! Stop moving! If you take a wrong turn, you'll put more walls between us. That will make it impossible for us to hear you."

Fisch's voice floated to them. "I've made a mess of things: I dropped the lantern, the light went out, it's getting colder, and I haven't eaten in centuries. Things are getting *very bad,* and I would like to admit that I am very scared!" There was a pause, then: "This is where things are going to end for me, isn't it? I'm going to die here, alone and cold and hungry, hearing your voices like you're ghosts."

"We're not ghosts. You're *fine*, stop panicking," Sybaline said, even as his panic seeped into her.

"I'm not panicking. I'm being *realistic.*"

"Then stop being realistic!" Nettle said.

Fisch's next words were too distanced to understand, small snippets of sound that were only murmurs.

"Fisch, *stop moving!*" Hurried, Sybaline stepped forward, trying to guess which way he went. "Nettle and I will come find *you*, but the only way we can do that is if you *stop moving.*"

Both Sybaline and Nettle leaned forward, trying to listen for Fisch's response, but when none came, they each turned to the other, alarm lining their eyes.

"He can't get lost and die. Not like this. I'll use magic." Sybaline reached for the magic. It collected, warm and comforting...to her right.

"I've already found him," Nettle said.

Horror clouded Sybaline's thoughts. She turned, raising

her lantern as she did. Molten light shoved back the shadows from Nettle's hair. Ginseng roots hung in limp clumps over her entire head, not just on a few strands like it had that morning.

"How's it look?" Nettle shook her head, grinning.

"That's not funny. *I* was the one who was supposed to use the magic."

"Why? Because you feel bad?" The smile fell from Nettle's face. "It's too late. It's already done. I used the magic, and I know where he is. Let's not let this opportunity go to waste because you feel guilty."

With that, Nettle turned and took the middle tunnel. She was gone for but a moment before appearing with a very disgruntled Fisch. Tears wound down his dirty face; the undersides of his eyes were puffy and stained with salted grime.

"I'm sorry," he said, his gaze cast to the ground. "You told me to stay put. I should've stayed put, but I thought I could look around for things we could use to insulate the house, like you said. Leaves or…or cornstalks. I wandered, and by the time I realized I'd walked into a tunnel, I didn't know how to get back."

"You were following a path," Nettle said, and shone her light on the ground where his muddy tracks cut along the trail Nettle and Sybaline had carved.

"I…what?" Fisch's voice, watery and broken, cracked.

"You didn't know?" Sybaline asked, already realizing that he hadn't. He'd probably never thought to look down and find his own tracks. Poor Fisch. "Herbert Fisch," she said, "you might've not stayed put, but I sure do hope you got around to thinking, because Nettle and I need to find a way out of this place, and we'd like to take you with us."

Fisch started crying again, great wrenching sobs neither Sybaline nor Nettle knew what to do with, and so they each took hold of Fisch's arms, and together, they all walked free from the tunnel.

CHAPTER 25

"If we break the water wall, we'll all drown!" Nettle shouted, not for the first time.

It was two full days later and they weren't any closer to figuring out how to escape the bubble, considering the *bubble* was the entire problem. It might have saved them from drowning in the rising tides or getting crushed by the lake above them, but now, it was the sole reason they couldn't escape.

The water on the ground that had once formed a thin layer of mud now covered their feet, meaning that they stayed wet and cold anytime they ventured off the porch, and the fog hovered constant, never blown away by wind or dried up by the sun. Parts of nature Sybaline had once found beautiful were now attempting to gulp them down.

They'd run the full gamut of ideas, always circling back to the main problem they had: escape required magic.

"If we poke a hole in the water wall—and I'm *not* saying that's even possible, Fisch—the entire thing will leak around us.

It'd be like air squeezing out of a balloon." Nettle set her hands on her hips, standing just like Wonder Woman or Superman or someone else who intended to save the day. "If all the air disappears out of our bubble, we'll die."

"Okay, okay," Fisch said. "I came up with a bad idea. All I was thinking is that we needed to change the pressure of the bubble."

"*We need to change the pressure of the bubble*," Nettle said, mimicking Fisch's voice, albeit pitched an octave too high.

"I don't sound like that," Fisch said.

"Herby-Herb, I'm mad right now."

"That doesn't mean you get to make fun of me."

"I'm making fun of what you *said*, there's a difference. You said, *We need to change the pressure of the bubble*." She looked at him with raised brows. "See?"

"Stop." Exhaustion made Sybaline's teeth ache, and so did stepping between Nettle and Fisch's bickering. Ever since Nettle had saved Fisch in the tunnel and then Fisch had tossed "science" and "engineering" and a whole lot of other gibberish at them as if neither of them had gone to school, they'd been fighting.

The problem is that the bubble is pushing out and the water is pushing in. Pressure between the two forces equalized.

We already know *this part*, said Nettle. *We've gone over it before.*

Fine, but we haven't gone over the part that if you want the bubble gone, you need the equalization gone. You've got to find a way to change the pressure. You've got to break the seal of the bubble. Then, maybe we could change its size. Maybe we could make it small, and we could all float to the surface!

Which led to this moment, with Nettle tossing up her arms and disappearing around the side of her house, likely to scrounge for food in her mother's garden, not that she would find much. The garden was truly dying. Not dying in the way plants did during winter, when leaves split from vines and crumbled against the ground, brittle and worn from a season of soaking up the sun. That sort of dying was only a *rest*, an *it's time to sleep*, an *I'll see you in a few months.* This dying was the sort of dying that happened when life bled from a rabbit snatched up by a fox, or the sort of dying trees did when shorn mid-trunk by a saw.

It wasn't a transfer, a shifting or a shaping, a choosing of the world to bury its life deep and wake again come another season. It was an ending, and it was an ending that would take Nettle, Marlys, Tevi, Fisch, and Sybaline with it, because it meant they wouldn't have a way to gather food. Soon, they would have nothing to eat, and the truth of it angered Nettle in a way that Sybaline hadn't known was possible. Every time she returned from the drowning, dying garden, it was with an expression Sybaline had never seen before.

"Desperate times," Sybaline murmured to herself.

"What?" asked Fisch.

"Nothing." She walked to where the axe lay inside the wheelbarrow and hefted it in her hands, fingers falling over the grooves where her daddy's hands had once wrapped. The silken wood felt like calm against her callused palms. "It's a magical barrier, Fisch. I would assume the only way through a magical barrier is by using magic. We can't chop a hole in the wall. It's too solid."

"Using magic will kill you."

"It'll *transform* me. That's not the same thing as dying." Sybaline stared at Fisch until a thin, watery film fell over her eyes. She blinked and blinked again, trying to dust it away. The magic *was* transforming her, and that transformation wasn't a life she wanted.

There's a third choice, Aunt Ethel had said long ago. *We can use our magic and stay.*

At one point, Sybaline had thought that transforming would be better than leaving the valley. She certainly didn't think that any longer. She hadn't understood what it would mean to transform in order to stay, but now that she did, she found it terrifying.

Setting the axe back in the wheelbarrow, she turned and peered through the open doorway to where Marlys and Tevi lay snuggled on the blankets.

Lethargic and sad, Tevi had spent the last days curled before the fire, and Marlys had taken to braiding and unbraiding her little sister's hair. *She misses the sun*, Marlys said the night before.

Sybaline missed the sun, too, but the *missing* had settled in Tevi in a different way than it had Sybaline. It made her words come slow and movements sluggish. The *missing* was woven into her body, a transformation, much in the same way that Sybaline's body was transforming into a tree.

"We need to get out," Sybaline said, watching as Marlys brushed her fingers through Tevi's hair. Their shadows danced along the floor behind them, cast up by the fire.

Fisch threw a rock at the barrier. It smacked against the wall in a place where the light didn't reach; the sound of it echoed back to them.

Sybaline leaned forward and pressed her hands to the bark of her. To the rough, wooden skin that marched up and over her knees. How deep did the tree parts of her run? Her muscles ached with it. Her joints distanced themselves from her body, as if they no longer wanted to be joints that hinged two moving parts of her, but instead were the Y between the branches of a tree, limbs sprouting in two different directions, unmoving but for a gentle sway.

She saw, suddenly, the way the rest of her life would go: The whole of her body would completely transform sooner rather than later. She would plant herself in the ground, feet burying deep, roots spreading into the earth. Her arms would stretch toward the sky, where the sun no longer dripped life-giving rays to the plants beneath the water. Her hair would twine into leaves and her breath would become the cells in the grains of wood.

Nettle would transform, too, all because Sybaline had turned tree and she'd had no other way to survive. Marlys and Tevi likely would as well, forced to make the decision because the people who were meant to protect them had failed.

Herbert Fisch would watch all of them disappear, and then he, alone, would discover which of the horrible ways he'd envisioned he would die: hypothermia or starvation.

And Sybaline's home would live forever inside this bubble of protected space until someday, someone would dive to the bottom of the lake. There, they would find the water wall and the bubble and inside it, the ghost town. Would anyone ever know that Sybaline and her friends lay inside this grave? Would her family ever understand what had happened?

Calm enveloped Sybaline. It was the magic, *always* the magic. Warm and engulfing and hungry—a sort of hunger she'd always needed, for she'd always needed something to live for. Now, she understood she needed to learn how to live for herself separate from the magic and the valley altogether.

She reached for it, and when she asked it to, the magic pooled against her hands. She pushed it out, letting it tangle with one of the water walls she'd made when she'd thought Tevi was a bear.

Distantly, Sybaline heard Nettle shouting at her. "*What are you doing?*"

But Sybaline didn't stop, because she knew the only way to leave the magic behind was to use it to escape. She took hold of the top of the wall where it met with the bubble and *pulled*.

The wall drew down, taking the bubble with it, except the bubble was too strong for her to tear, and it slipped from her grip. She felt the magic slide away from her, and the bubble snapped back into place. Taking a huge breath, she collected her strength and used all of the magic her body could hold, reaching out for *all* of the places *all* of the water walls met with the bubble, for surely she could put a tiny tear in at least one spot in the surface of the bubble. All she needed to do was change the pressure. Stop the equalization between the bubble pushing out and the lake pushing in.

Strength flooded her, sudden and reassuring, and she pulled with the magic again. This time, she felt the bubble give the slightest, felt a tiny seam open in the bubble above.

"I did it." Sybaline looked up, expecting to see the barrier far above shifting and growing smaller, but instead, all she saw was darkness.

Pure, unfiltered black, just like always.

"I didn't do it?" she whispered, heart sinking into an inky blackness of its own.

"No!" came Fisch's shout from behind her.

"I'm sorry," Sybaline said, hiding her face. "I thought I made a hole in the bubble. I wanted to change the pressure."

Something thumped to the ground behind her.

"Nettle!" Marlys screamed.

"You killed her!" Tevi shouted.

Sybaline twisted best she could—all of her body, from her torso down, had stiffened while working magic—and found Nettle laying in the bright light of her home.

Sybaline tried to disentangle her legs from the awkward position in which she'd folded herself. When she pushed herself up to stand, her knees only bent the slightest. Pain radiated up her legs and into her hips as she tried to force them to move. She hauled herself to where Fisch and Marlys and Tevi crouched over Nettle. Ribbons of white spread down Nettle's face, streaking over her nose and into her open eyes and across the smooth skin of her cheeks. *Ginseng root.*

Nettle must've joined Sybaline in working magic just now, and it had hurried along her transformation. While Sybaline's transformation had begun in her feet, Nettle's had begun in her head.

Sybaline tried to crouch, but all she could do was fall, and so she dropped and lay next to Nettle, her fingers pressing to Nettle's neck.

"Is she dead?" Marlys whispered, hands hovering over Nettle.

"She still has a pulse," Sybaline said.

"Maybe she's just unconscious," Fisch said, who stooped on Nettle's other side.

The smallest drop of water splashed against Sybaline's forehead and slid to the end of her nose, clinging for a moment before falling off and soaking into the damp between Nettle and her.

"*What?*" Fisch raised his open hand, palm up. A teardrop of liquid balanced on his skin, right over the lifeline that crossed his palm.

Another drop fell and hit Sybaline's shoulder. Wondrous, she felt at the damp place on her sleeve, saying, "It's raining."

"It *can't* rain here." Fisch's voice tipped up in pitch at the end, almost as if he were asking a question. "There are no weather patterns here. No clouds. No storms. No rain. Weather doesn't exist inside the bubble!"

Sybaline tilted her face toward the darkness where Nettle's

houselights didn't reach. She kept her eyes peeled, and *there*, another drop fell and then another, zooming through the light to tumble onto the already saturated ground.

"It's not raining." She held her hands toward the place where the sky should exist. "The barrier is *leaking*."

CHAPTER 26

"Nettle must've helped me with the magic." Sybaline picked up Nettle's feet while Fisch grabbed under her armpits. "I knew we couldn't chop a hole in the side of the bubble, but I remembered when we pulled on the water walls that form the tunnels between my house and the gristmill, they pulled down. It felt like the bubble would tear. I thought I could make a tiny tear and release pressure from the whole thing."

Together, they hoisted Nettle under the porch, where they were protected from the water that rained from the sky. The thin drips fell in a sheen, a hazy curtain that separated the house from the darkness. It was too cold for any of them to afford getting wet.

Tevi squatted at Nettle's side and held a hand over her mouth. "She's breathing. How do we wake her up?"

Marlys said, "We don't. She's gone."

"She's not *gone*," Sybaline said, fierce. "Whatever she's turned into, she's not completely transformed. Not yet." Her cousin's rooty hair stood out in a chaos of directions, and her untanned skin faded from white to the cream of ginseng, threaded through with spindly, brown fibers. Sybaline turned to Fisch, not able to look longer at Nettle. She couldn't cope with the anxiety that swarmed inside her. "I don't understand what's happening. I thought I was tearing just a small hole in the bubble. Why is it raining here?"

"Maybe you made more than one tear by mistake?" Fisch patted down the roots of Nettle's hair, then tucked his hands inside his pockets. "Maybe when you tore the bubble, a bunch of tiny rips went through the whole thing, kind of like when a flag starts fraying in the wind."

"That doesn't make any sense!" Sybaline stared at Fisch, aghast at the suggestion he was making—that she didn't know how to use the magic. "You don't understand how magic works if you're saying that."

"I never pretended to."

"I would only have done that if I'd made a mistake. If I'd…" Sybaline trailed off, words dying straight in her throat. She'd made plenty of mistakes with magic while down here, and it'd always happened because she was desperate, because she didn't sit still long enough to figure out a plan before she went ahead and did something.

Sybaline shifted on her feet, wanting to sit beside Nettle

but knowing that if she sat, she might not get back up again. Last time she'd had to stand back up had been difficult enough. She didn't think she could do it again.

Marlys asked, "If the sky keeps leaking, how long will it take to flood?"

Fisch tucked his chin to his chest and sucked on his teeth for a moment before saying, "It depends on if the bubble holds. It might collapse before it floods."

Sybaline stilled. The world stilled. The porch held the echo of Fisch's words and the threat of the bubble collapsing in one swoop.

"The small tears could widen. The water could force a giant hole through. It could thin the edge of the bubble."

"Fisch."

"Since the pressure is seeping away, the entire barrier could disappear in one go, unannounced. We'd be crushed fla—"

"*Fisch!*" Sybaline's voice, turned shrill and sharp, stopped Fisch midsentence. "I get it. I understand. It's bad! You don't have to spell it out."

"Sorry," Fisch said.

"How do we get out of this mess?"

"We stick to the plan."

"Except now, we don't have Nettle. *I* don't have Nettle. There's no one here to help me."

"I'm here." Fisch's hair, grungy and ragged about his ears, hung low over his brow, making it nearly impossible for Sybaline to see his expression.

"Thank you," Sybaline said, meaning it. She hadn't wanted his friendship before, hadn't thought him worthy of friendship, but now, she knew how wrong she'd been.

"I'm here too," Marlys said.

"Me too," Tevi said.

Sybaline steeled herself. "If I'm going to shrink the bubble down small enough for us to try to float out of the lake, I'll probably only have one chance to try it." After that, her entire body would probably transform.

"We'll take care of Nettle while you work magic," Fisch said.

Sybaline nodded, realizing they couldn't stay at the gristmill any longer. The mill was hundreds of feet below the lake, that meant hundreds of feet of water she would have to push them through. If she wanted this plan to succeed, they needed to be as close to the surface of the lake as they could get. "For this to work, we need to climb to higher ground. We need to get to Papaw's hill."

Sybaline grabbed the wheelbarrow from the side of the house, rolling it through the sloshing mud and to the porch, where

Fisch was busy laying supplies out of reach of the rain. Already, water slicked the insides of the barrow.

"We need to line it with something," Marlys said. "I'm not making my sister lay in a wet wheelbarrow."

"I'll get our blankets," Tevi said, rushing back inside.

"We'll dress in layers. All of the ones we have," Sybaline said, while knowing the more her legs continued to transform, the less she would need the warmth of clothes. After all, trees weren't bothered by the cold. All they did in winter was shed their autumn-wear and head straight to bed.

Fisch ran into the house, with Sybaline stumbling behind. Sweat chilled the skin along her still-human sides as she struggled to move. Hauling herself up the steps, she saw Fisch and Marlys collecting what few clothes they had left. Marlys held up a cloak and said it was for Nettle to keep her warm while she lay inside the wheelbarrow.

Fisch then scrounged through the living quarters, pausing by the fireplace that had long since burned free of wood. From beside it, he took up the silver flashlight he'd had in the theater. Tucking it into a pocket, he glanced at the food they'd lined along the mantel.

"Hurry," Sybaline said, impatient.

Fisch said, "What if we need other supplies than what we can take now?"

"Either we manage to escape the lake, and we won't need supplies; or we don't escape, and we still won't need supplies."

Fisch's hand hovered over a can of beans. He closed his fist and started to tuck it away, but then in a rush, he swiped the can up and stuck it into his pocket, saying, "Just in case."

He slung his pack over his shoulder, then joined Sybaline at the door. There, they took up positions on either end of Nettle, with Marlys and Tevi at her shoulders. They hoisted her up and, jolting down the stairs with Sybaline's uneven gait, walked into the strange rain. They settled Nettle inside, propping her head at what looked to be a not-too-uncomfortable angle, and then covered her with the cloak.

"I'll lead," Sybaline said. "Fisch will push the wheelbarrow. Marlys and Tevi, walk between us."

Fisch pulled a makeshift hood over his head and ducked down, wrapping his hands around the handles.

Sybaline clambered back up the steps, the need to hurry filling every fiber of her body. She took up the lantern she'd set by the door, the flame dancing inside.

"Are you all ready?" Sybaline asked.

"No." Fisch steadied his grasp on the wheelbarrow, his feet disappearing into the water that pooled along the ground.

Sybaline took in a steadying breath, said, "Me neither," then turned out the lights of the gristmill, casting the world into darkness. Small points of light made by their lanterns glowed against the crushing black.

She stumbled down the steps, walked past Fisch and her cousins, and plunged down the path that she and Nettle had carved through the woods.

CHAPTER 27

The dripping rain began to fall in sheets halfway to Sybaline's house. It slithered down the back of her cloak, bumping along the ridges of her spine, and coming to the place on her legs where her skin was no longer skin. The numb feeling had crept up her hips and to her lower back. Her joints creaked as she walked, muscles sliding along wooden bone, grating in a way that made her flinch.

"Which way?" Fisch asked from where he stood in front of Sybaline.

She and Fisch had to switch positions after he'd run into tree roots and dumped Nettle out of the barrow. It turned out there was a learning curve to racing through the woods with a wheelbarrow, and Fisch didn't have the time to learn. Marlys and Tevi had offered to drive, but it weighed too much for them to safely push. Now, Sybaline held tight to the handles, balancing it best she could as they made their way through the forest.

"The path is gone," Fisch said.

On his other side, Marlys patrolled the wall, bending low with her lantern, the light sputtering among the raindrops. "It's too muddy to tell which way the path leads."

"Where do we walk?" Tevi asked.

Except Sybaline didn't know. They stood surrounded by a ring of black. Rain slid down the edges of the barrier, liquid water glistening along solid water. She tried to orient herself, to know innately where her home was, to ignore the walls around her and pretend the world was as it used to be.

She'd never had to think how to get home before, but now, with her body changed and the rain dampening her senses and the echoing of the barrier, she had no idea where to go. Panic stretched its claws through her.

"*Sybaline?*" Tevi's voice shook.

"I don't know." She clutched the handles of the wheelbarrow.

"You don't know?" Fisch spun toward her, lantern held too high, and it blinded her. She ducked her head, closing her eyes against the light. "How can you *not* know? Are we lost?"

"We're not lost. We're...here. We're right here." She pointed at the ground. "I don't know how to get from here to there." She pointed to where she guessed her home to be.

"This is as bad as when I was lost the other day."

"It's not nearly as bad. This time, you have a can of beans," Sybaline said.

"You sound like Nettle."

"Someone's got to tell the jokes." She glanced at her cousin, who slept on, oblivious to the trouble Sybaline had gotten them into.

Fisch ran a hand through his damp hair, then, gingerly, he handed his lantern to Marlys and took out his flashlight. He flicked it on and pressed its end to the barrier. The dim beam of light passed into the depths, turning a shade of green that reminded Sybaline of leaves collecting atop puddles of water and rotting in the uneven temperatures of fall.

"You can't see through the wall, Fisch," Sybaline said.

"No, but we can hear through it. Sound carries in water. We might be able to hear the right direction to go."

Exhausted, Sybaline leaned her weight onto the wheelbarrow, taking pressure off her legs. "That makes no sense."

Fisch pressed his ear to the barrier and, using the flashlight, tapped against the wall. He gave no reaction, but after a moment, stepped farther down the wall and repeated the process. Sybaline stood in place, shivers marching over her arms but not touching her legs, and watched as he shifted up and down the tunnel, going from one end to the other, moving far enough into the darkness that at one point, she lost sight of him.

Enough time passed that Sybaline began to ache with cold,

the sort that went from chattering teeth to a locked jaw. The sound of Fisch's footsteps arrived before he did.

"I think I've got it." His light illuminated his weak smile.

Sybaline pushed the wheelbarrow forward, following Fisch without question.

"The parts of the wall that lead toward openings sound tinnier. We're looking for the next opening."

Sweat and rain mingled to stain the handles of the wheelbarrow, which turned slick against Sybaline's grip as she followed after Fisch. The darkness expanded around them, but all at once, the feeling of open air, of the world widening and yawning around them flooded her. She broke into a trot after Fisch, her stumbling legs trying to run through the water and the woods without bending at the knees.

"I know this place!" she shouted, spotting an apple tree; a smell of rot and decay drifted up from the fruit now covering the ground underneath it. "Keep right, Fisch. We need to stay away from my home and head toward the hill."

They needed higher ground, and the highest place Sybaline knew of that hadn't drowned beneath the lake was beyond her house.

Marlys and Tevi whooped and ran in front of them, leading the way.

"Almost there." She steered the wheelbarrow, wincing

when the back of Nettle's head bumped against the steel barrow after rolling over a large rock.

Fisch kept running, holding the lantern in one hand and the flashlight in the other, illuminating their way. Light from the lantern bobbed at his feet, flashing over fallen trees and moss turned brown and dead. The thin, yellowing glow from the flashlight spun into the distance, tossing up more shadows than good illumination. It played tricks on Sybaline's eyes. Branches as fingers. Trunks as long-limbed monsters. Pine needles as the razor-thin teeth of nightmare-beasts. Fog as a veil to the afterworld. Water as a wolf gorging itself on a kill.

"Here!" Sybaline shouted, and she slowed the wheelbarrow, bringing it to a halt, just as she saw Fisch trip and fall on his knees. He landed in the place where the earth gave way to a sharp incline.

Marlys and Tevi had known the hill was coming, and they'd flown up it, flinging their bodies toward Papaw's tree.

Gently, Sybaline set down the wheelbarrow and went to stand by Nettle's shoulders. She brushed rainwater off the ropy strands of ginseng beside her face.

"How are we going to carry her?" Fisch asked.

Sybaline grimaced and tried to bend one of her legs, the frozen knee making the movement impossible. "You're going to have to. I'm going to have a hard enough time making the climb on my own."

225

"I won't make it up the hill carrying her! I can't walk up hills on my own, much less while holding someone else."

"You can do it, Fisch. You have to. We'll tie Nettle to you, and I'll help push."

They balanced Nettle on Fisch's back, and using the blanket that Nettle had lain on in the barrow, they made a sling and tied it around both Nettle and Fisch. He stood with his toes at the bottom of the rise and his fingers digging into the soil that rose at a sharp angle up, up, and *up*.

Sybaline braced herself, standing at the bottom of the rise, one hand on the small of Nettle's back. She looked up at the place where the top of the hill disappeared into the murky darkness. Somewhere up there, Papaw's tree spread its limbs into the open air of the bubble.

"Let's go," Fisch said.

CHAPTER 28

Sybaline clawed her way up the hill, hands digging into the flaking dirt that steadily drank up the rain. She jammed her feet into the ground, no longer able to bend her knees and push with the strength of her legs. She kept her head ducked low to keep her eyes safe from the grass that fell over her, shucked out of place by Fisch's tread. He climbed somewhere above her in the darkness. Only occasionally did she hear muttered words spit out on an exhale. Her own lungs, too strained to allow her to form questions, burned, and she couldn't ask Fisch how he was doing.

She hadn't been able to help him; she was having too difficult a time helping herself. But Marlys and Tevi had run back. Holding tight to Nettle's arms, they all marched uphill.

Sybaline had fallen behind, her gasping, horrible breaths not enough to push her faster and keep up with Fisch. Her fingers dug into the hill, small hooks sinking into the dirt that'd begun to turn to mud. It ran down the side of the hill and caked the front of her dress and toes of her boots. The heaviness of it dragged against her momentum, but still she pushed. Nettle was turning into a plant, and Marlys and Tevi were going to be left alone, and Fisch was going to die, and it all was Sybaline's fault. In desperation, she hoisted her stubborn body upward, closing her eyes and gritting her teeth, until her entire existence narrowed to the small movements that brought her closer to the top of the rise and closer to the lake's surface.

"*Ahh!*" Fisch shouted, then: a thump, a sigh, a body dropping itself onto the ground.

Sybaline didn't dare let her heart believe the top was close. She dragged her tree limb legs up the slanted earth and understood why trees never bothered to uproot themselves and find new homes. Perhaps that was why the magic had decided to turn her into a tree: She'd always been unwilling to leave. This was the choice that had always been open to her—stay and bury her roots in the valley.

She reached up, but instead of meeting with slanted earth, she met with air and fell forward. She crawled the last two steps and collapsed beside Fisch at the top of the steep hill.

Fisch sat up and shone his flashlight around. The weak beam passed through the dripping rain and shone a spotlight on the upturned dirt of the empty graves, black and shadowed against the grains of grass surrounding them. The light swung around, illuminating the small, flat-topped hill and then landing on Papaw, who stood proud and tall, long branches stretching wildly in all directions.

"That's your grandpa?" he asked, for Marlys had told him all about Papaw on their way to the cemetery.

"It's our papaw." Tevi slid her palm against his bark. "I never met him when he was a person though."

"He seems like he would have been very nice," said Fisch. "Now what do we do?"

Sybaline rolled over onto her back and looked toward the lake above her. The heaviness of it pushed her into the valley floor, told her she might as well not try, but despite the pressure, she said, "Now I have to be brave, even though I am very, *very* scared."

That fear turned restless inside her. It nested in her lungs, a hive for wasps, and they buzzed and buzzed in the space between her ribs. That fear had been birthed when the government man first arrived years ago, telling her family their home would be gone soon, and it'd never left: fear for Poppa at war, fear for her brother at the dam, fear for her brother who never wanted to stay, fear for Momma at the sadness that showed in her face when she thought no one was looking, and fear for not fitting in wherever Sybaline would move…fear for losing the one thing she'd thought made her *her.*

She'd bent beneath that fear and had allowed it to grow.

She'd fed it with the choices she'd made, guided by uncertainty and the looming unknown. Now, she could still be scared, but she could also choose to be brave. Her fear would *not* make her choices for her.

Sybaline glanced at her human hands, knowing full well that what she was about to attempt might transform them altogether. She and Nettle had done the hard part, earlier. They'd released the pressure of the barrier that contained them, but what she had to do now was find a way to collapse the wall. Collapse it and wrap it about them in a much, *much* smaller version of the bubble she'd first made. It would be a tiny bubble that would only hold the five of them.

But to do that, she had to be willing to make the terrible choice of saying goodbye to the valley, because saying goodbye was the only way to save her cousins and Fisch.

In, out, she slid air through her lungs. She said hello to her fear and the way it rattled inside her body. She told herself she was brave. Breathing this thought, she reached out with her hands. The magic pooled against her skin.

She raised a water wall around them in a small circle, allowing it to bend above in a miniature version of the bubble. Then, she hooked into the small holes she'd torn through the larger bubble earlier and *pulled*. It came apart, soft as a leaf mid-storm, tugged from its tree.

A rush of a waterfall, the whistle of a train, the screaming wind of a tornado drowned out the screams of Fisch, Marlys, and Tevi. The big bubble popped and the entire lake fell inward. Pressure built behind Sybaline's eyes and against her ears, as *whomp*! Sound exploded around them and then stopped all at once. Her ears popped and sharp pain sliced through her head.

She whimpered and raised one hand to her ear, where a trickle of liquid ran down her lobe.

"Too much pressure," gasped Fisch. His voice came to her, thin and distant, as if he were on the opposite end of a crackling phone line.

She opened her eyes to darkness, her chest caving in with despair. Black lake water had devoured her valley. It encompassed all the parts of the home she'd wanted to save.

She turned her head and saw Fisch, who gripped his flashlight to his chest, its beam shining against his chin. He rasped, "That was horrible. That was... That would've been death by crushing force. It would've been instantaneous."

Sybaline glanced around their new, small bubble. "Do you think our idea will work?"

"Air wants to rise, which means that hopefully our little bubble will want to float to the surface," Fisch said. "It probably just needs a good shove with your magic to get going."

Sybaline, still laying on the ground with the lining of the

bubble beneath her, didn't dare move her legs to discover how much of her body had changed while she'd worked magic to pop the bubble. There was only so much fear she was willing to confront head-on in one day.

Tevi's small hand twined around her wrist. She whispered, "You can do it."

Gathering the magic to her, Sybaline lined the bottom of the bubble with her power and built up the strength to *push*.

CHAPTER 29

Sybaline had created the bubble by pushing back the water, pushing back the outside world, and pushing back the life she thought she didn't want.

Now, she pushed *toward* something—toward her family, toward safety, toward the sun and the wind and the secret smile Momma gave when talking about Poppa.

The water of the lake parted as their small bubble rose through the sludge and headed toward the surface. She imagined they were inside the air bubble of a giant who slept beneath the valley.

"It's working." Fisch pointed his flashlight at the barrier and cupped his hands around his eyes, trying to see out.

Beside her, Tevi's nervous breath shuddered as she exhaled, and she gripped Sybaline's wrist harder. Creeping numbness spread through Sybaline's bones, through her blood that seemed to thicken, moving sap-like through her veins.

Push, and *push,* and...*push.* She kept pushing with her magic, trying to shove their bubble faster to the surface.

"I see light!" Fisch stood. He stretched his arms above his head. His fingertips pressed against the top of the bubble.

Light fuzzed on the other side of the barrier. It drew closer, as if Sybaline were rubbing sleep from her eyes and blinking up at the weak morning sun.

Hope bloomed in Sybaline's chest.

Fisch shouted, pumping his fists in the air. Marlys joined him, reaching toward the surface of the lake and the outside world that was just a moment away.

All at once, her magic *disappeared.*

The warmth around her, inside, *beneath* her rocketed away. The bubble continued floating up for a moment, pushed onward by the momentum she'd built, but then their movement stopped. They hovered, suspended in the water.

"Why are we stopping, Sybaline?" Fisch asked, his voice breaking through the panic that had begun to rise in her. "Why aren't we going up anymore?"

She sucked air through her nose, nostrils whistling with the force of her inhalation. *Breathe through it,* Momma whispered through her thoughts. *Breathe through it. Your body will get used to not having the magic. You are not dying; it only feels like it.*

"Sybaline! *What's happening?*" Fisch shouted.

"I can't push us anymore. The magic is gone," she said, her cheek turned and pressed to the freezing bottom of the bubble. The valley floor, so far below them, sung with magic, but up here in the middle of the lake, no magic existed. Right now, they floated in what had once been the sky, and no magic that she knew of had ever lived in the sky.

"Sybaline?" Tevi's hushed whisper filled the small space in which they existed.

Their bubble sunk. They drifted downward slow, *slow* as dandelion seeds falling through the air, the wind having paused in its breathless rush. They slid through the murk, what little light from above that had grown dimmed as they dropped away.

The magic returned as soon as they neared the earth. Warmth enveloped her skin and lit her from within, but she didn't grab for it. She didn't hold it close to her body. She didn't try to harness it and attempt the push a second time. She lay still, the heavy, wooden bones of her body weighing her down.

CHAPTER 30

This time, Fisch didn't ask, *What do we do now?* And Sybaline didn't say, *I don't know.* Marlys didn't ask, *What's the next idea?* And Tevi didn't say, *I could use magic and help.* They didn't look at one another or find comfort in the fact they were together. They didn't think or plan or buy hope for another attempt.

They stayed where they were, and they existed.

They rested in exactly the same spot where they'd started, on the hill next to Papaw.

They grasped the edges of fear and wrapped it about their shoulders, a blanket heavier than all the tons of water above them.

Sybaline folded her fingertips into the skin of her hips and stomach and found not skin at all, but the unforgiving flesh of a laurel tree. The transformation would complete itself soon. She knew what would come next as certain as she knew her own name. Knew what taking this final step would mean for her.

Knew her last choice would be her *best* choice. She said, "I know I can't push us all out, but I think I can push *you* out."

Beside her, Fisch sat, folding his legs beneath him. Marlys sat, too, no longer jumping and cheering. Tevi crawled into Marlys's lap, then reached over and took hold of Nettle's hand.

"The farther we got from the valley floor, the farther I got from the magic, until my link to it disappeared." Sybaline's fingers tightened against her wooden skin. "When I'm on the earth, and I'm linked to the magic, I have more power. I should be able to push all of you out. But I'll have to stay."

"No," Fisch whispered.

"You're all here because of me. Nettle is transformed because of me. Let me save you."

"*No,*" Tevi said, forcefully.

"We won't leave you alone down here," Marlys said.

"This is my choice. Don't you dare take that away from me," Sybaline said, echoing what Nettle had once told her. With a rush, she grabbed up the magic and *pushed*. A thin barrier drew between them, cutting their bubble in two with Sybaline on one side and Nettle, Marlys, Tevi, and Fisch on the other.

Inside their little bubble, Tevi screamed. She stood and pounded her fists against the wall. The claps of sound ricocheted against the small space of Sybaline's bubble, but of course, Tevi couldn't get through.

Tears leaked from her eyes, but she refused to close them or look away.

Push, push, push. Sybaline drew magic from the earth and shoved it against the small bubble her family and friends lived inside. She pushed them up and away.

Toward the break between water and sky.

Toward the fresh air that buoyed birds into clouds.

Toward books and movies and family and friends and running barefoot through the woods, winding between trees and streams of light, and then standing frozen in a sea of wildflowers.

She pushed their bubble toward the surface of the lake. Toward *life*.

CHAPTER 31

"Papaw," Sybaline said into the darkness. Fisch had taken the flashlight with him, and they hadn't lit a lantern for Sybaline; they'd never assumed they'd separate. The limbs of Papaw's tree scratched against the edge of her bubble, shifting with the tides of the lake, its sound a tinny reverberation against her ears. "How do I do this?"

How do I live at the bottom of the lake?

How do I allow myself to transform into a laurel tree?

How do I make peace with my choices?

How do you try again? said something that felt an awful lot like Papaw's voice inside her.

Sybaline turned her head so she faced Papaw's direction. Though she couldn't see him, she could feel him.

Try again. No matter what, you can always, always *try again.*

She heard the words in her mind as if Papaw had spoken them, except, too, it sounded just like what Nettle would have said, what Momma would have said, what any of her aunts would have said.

You're asking yourself the wrong questions, said the wisdom of the people who loved her, because as always, Sybaline was asking herself the wrong questions.

Inside her fear, she had asked: *Who will I become if I leave this place?* What she should have asked was: *Who will I become if I stay?*

This was the answer to that question: Sybaline *wasn't* staying. She wouldn't lay down and give up. That wasn't an option.

With her feet numb and legs transformed and hips wooden and torso heavy and ribs the same thickness and density as a sapling's trunk, she gathered magic beneath her. Perhaps with the smaller bubble and her lighter weight, she could send herself close enough to the top of the lake that the bubble would float to the surface on its own.

No matter if she stayed or if she tried once more to leave, she would become a tree, but at least this way, she would transform knowing she'd done her best, knowing she hadn't drowned beneath her fear.

She headed toward this last change, said goodbye to the valley that had built magic of her blood and goodbye to her Papaw, who had gifted her strength. And once again, she *pushed.*

CHAPTER 32

Up through the sediment. Up through the flotsam. Up through the viscous thickness of the water Sybaline went. She tightened her hold around the magic, and the transformation of her body turned from a creep to a rush, numbing each bone in her skeleton.

With the lake newly flooded, it was filled with dirt; it would take a long while for the muck to settle and free itself from the water. As before, light appeared above her. Before her connection to the magic could sever altogether, she stopped pushing and paused.

You are brave, Sybaline Shaw, she told herself.

She grasped at the warm magic, and her arms, tingling with sleep, turned into the curved knobs of burls at her side. With the magic, she found the walls of the bubble, grabbed hold of the seam where the edges had come together. Pushing her magic into this weakness, she tore.

Water rushed in.

CHAPTER 33

The collapse of the bubble around Sybaline popped her ears. Water hurtled against her skin, between her toes, around the swirls of her hair. But, of course, her skin, her toes, her hair didn't mind. These parts of her body didn't mind, because these parts weren't human. All that was left of her human body was her face: her eyes and nose and mouth.

Somewhere above her, light glinted against motes in the water. How far away was the surface? Twenty feet? *Thirty* feet? Thirty-five?

The warmth of the sun didn't quite reach her. It lit the edges of her clothes and the bubbles that escaped her nose. She thought of the water invading her lungs, of *drowning is supposed to be a very peaceful way to die*. She held her breath and became desperate, lungs begging to turn into teeth to gobble down anything—air, water, *anything*. When her jaws tried to un-pry, she found they had fastened shut. They had turned *tree*. Even this part of her had transformed too.

The lake gripped her tree body. The light above her glowed, brighter and brighter, drawing close.

She was *floating*.

Her tree limbs, buoyant in the water, levitated through the lake toward the surface. As she rose, darkness ribboned the edges of her eyes. Unconsciousness ate away at her mind.

She was out of air.

Darkness more complete than that at the bottom of the lake caved in her vision. The world looked as if she were walking into a tunnel, black sliding over her eyes.

She thought, *thank you* to the valley beneath her, *thank you* to her family and friends, and *thank you* to the beautiful life she lived, and—

"*Sybaline*," said Nettle.

Cool air brushed her skin at the same time that her mind fell into deep, dark sleep.

CHAPTER 34

Warm hands closed over Sybaline's cheeks, over her wrists, over her shoulders. They touched the wooden parts of her and pressed against her mouth from which puffed small breaths of air.

"*Shhh*," whispered a voice, and this sent shivers through Sybaline, for it was a *shhh* she knew from when she was little and couldn't sleep for the nightmares that plagued her. A *shhh* that was whispered to settle her fear.

"*Shhh*," Momma murmured.

Desperate, aching love rushed through Sybaline, because even if she'd turned into a tree, she was with Momma. It was okay. She was okay. She was with family.

"*Shhh*."

Half-sob, half-whimper, a groan came from Sybaline's throat. Her lips twitched.

"My sweet girl." Momma wrapped her hand around Sybaline's.

Prickles started in the tips of her fingers, as if Momma

stuck her sewing needle against Sybaline's skin. Sybaline flinched, her hand spasming in Momma's grasp.

"I'm so sorry," Momma said.

Momma had no reason to be sorry, though. *Sybaline* did. Sybaline mewled, the cry of a baby or a cat, sudden pain scouring her skin. The relief that had stormed within her moments ago and had made her begin to cry turned into confusion, and her cry turned to one of fire. Her body rushed with heat, as if she'd been skewered with a hot iron or been stuck inside a burning hearth.

"It hurts. I'm sure it hurts." Momma's words cut through the pain of it. "It's the magic leaving your body. Backward transformation is a bad sort of pain."

Sybaline's jaw unhinged, and she sucked in a mouthful of air, dragging it deep into her lungs and belly. A real, full sob escaped her.

"You're okay, Syb," said a new voice, a not-her-momma's voice, *Nettle's* voice. "It hurts real awful for a bit, but it'll go away. You're coming back to life, is all. Sometimes living hurts."

Sybaline cried a different sort of cry now, because she'd been sure she'd killed Nettle. If she was hearing Nettle's voice, that meant not only was she alive, but she wasn't turning into a ginseng root any longer.

Another set of sobs cut through Sybaline's own, ones she'd

only heard once before on the night after Poppa left for war. Momma cried as she sat above Sybaline, and it made Sybaline swallow down her own pain. She wondered if Momma had been feeling the same agony that Syb had been over the last weeks.

Sybaline had made Momma feel like that, and she hadn't thought twice about it.

"I'm sorry," Sybaline whispered. The needles in her skin faded, burying deeper within her, pricking at her bones as they went from her chest to her hips to her thighs and calves. They pierced through the numbness of her feet. "I didn't mean to hurt you."

Momma cupped her chin with both hands and pressed a kiss to her forehead. Sybaline felt the kiss, not as if it were against her bark skin, but against the real skin she'd had days before.

"Why is this happening?" Sybaline asked. Slowly, the edges of her body were thawing out. Her eyelids blinked open, and Momma's blurred image appeared above her, wrinkles and gray hair and all.

"It never occurred to me to tell you, because it never occurred to me that you'd use magic in such a way," Momma said. "Transformations can be reversed if you leave the valley. You can never go back home, though, Sybaline. You'll transform right quick if you do."

"But...Bo? Aunt Ethel?"

"Neither Bo nor Ethel wanted to live anyplace but in our valley. It was worth it for them. They chose to live half-transformed."

Aunt Ethel's deep voice came from somewhere behind Sybaline. "As soon as I left the valley, the vines on my shoulders disappeared. They're gone, though in a strange way, I miss them."

Sybaline thought she understood what Aunt Ethel meant. The vines had been a tangible part of the valley that lived in her, and now, they were gone. If Aunt Ethel ever returned to the magic, she'd get her vines back, but for Sybaline, *all* of her would transform.

There was no way Sybaline would ever walk back the way from which she'd come. She'd fed her fear so long it'd made all her problems worse. It'd turned the place she loved into a thing made of horror and hunger. That had been her fault. She took responsibility for it.

"It sure took you long enough to come out of the lake," said one of her brothers.

Sybaline flinched, turning where she lay to peer around for the speaker. She craned her head back and found not one of her brothers but *both of them*. They leaned against the truck Cedric had borrowed to help move Momma.

"We knew you were down there," Benjamin said, "but we had no way to get to you."

"The aunts tried to use their magic to get beneath the lake, but of course, they didn't have any up here," Cedric said.

"All we could do was wait for you to get yourself out." Momma helped Sybaline sit up. "I realized you weren't at Granddaddy Neal's when I never received a return letter from you after the one I sent. Cedric drove me over there straight-away, but, of course, Wooline wasn't at Granddaddy Neal's. She'd gone to Ethel's. Once I got to Ethel's, we realized pretty quick what you all had done. We knew you two must have stayed in the valley and that Marlys and Tevi had run off to find you."

"The Larks are stubborn people." Aunt Ethel stepped into view, and Sybaline saw that indeed, no rumples formed beneath the shoulders of her dress where the vines had once grown.

Sybaline had been stubborn.

Aunt Ethel snorted. "I told you all there was a third choice! Use our magic and stay. Our girls proved to us how true that was."

"And how dumb it was," said Nettle. She sat on the opposite side of the fire. Tevi lay beside her, fast asleep, her face turned toward the sun high above. On Nettle's other side was Marlys, who was busy sharing food with Fisch.

"I shouldn't have stayed in the valley," Sybaline said, looking Momma full in the face.

"You made the best choice you could make, at the time," said Momma. "Everyone looks back on their life and knows where they made mistakes. I've made plenty of them myself."

Momma didn't blink or waver, and Sybaline wondered what sort of mistakes Momma was thinking on from her own life. What sort of regrets did she have? Someday soon, Sybaline would ask.

"You know I'm going to have to tell your poppa what you did," Momma said.

Sybaline's jaw dropped open. "But—"

"Oh no, no buts. No arguing. He's got to know." Momma brushed away the tears that fell down Sybaline's cheeks. "*But* I think we can probably wait until he gets home. You'll help me tell him."

Sybaline nodded, knowing that telling the story of what she'd done was her responsibility.

Her soaked dress pushed up against her calves, revealing the last of the backward transformation of rough bark to smooth skin. The grains and fibers of the laurel tree withdrew down her shins, the ring of leaves that had encircled her ankles absorbed into her skin, disappearing altogether, as if they'd never been there. The slow washing away of her mistakes erased all Sybaline's words—whatever else she could say to explain what she'd done. Now, all she wanted was the warmth of Momma's hand on her back, supporting her.

She looked around, finding that they sat in a clearing surrounded by trees with a warm fire burning in the center near her feet. Not far off, small waves sloshed across the surface of the lake. With the sun above, the dark water reflected the evergreens that lined the water's edge. All along the marshy shoreline, trees poked free from the lake, their branches waving as the current tugged them every which way. The sight of it sickened her, and she turned away.

Auntie Wooline and Aunt Ethel cooked up a storm over the fire, with everyone joining in to eat: Cedric, Benjamin, Momma and Sybaline, Nettle and Marlys and Tevi, and of course, Herbert Fisch.

Nettle moved so she sat beside Sybaline, a blanket thrown around both their shoulders. Across from them, Fisch criss-crossed his legs and leaned close to the fire, his hands held dangerously close to the flames. His hair was damp and clean for the first time in weeks, though it still stuck out at the strangest of angles, as if he'd truly gotten in a fight with a bear. His mother, when he finally got to her, would have trouble dragging a comb through it, and she very well might cut it off altogether.

Sybaline couldn't picture him without the ragged hair she'd gotten to know. Truth be told, she couldn't picture her life without him at all.

"You'll stay with our family until we get hold of yours," Momma said.

Fisch nodded, gaze not straying from the fire. "You were right, you know, Sybaline. The mountains weren't here for me to play in. You were right, too, in that they're beautiful. Beautiful and terrible and scary, and I feel like I know myself better since living among them. I wish I'd figured that out without having to nearly die, though." He glanced up, his face tilting toward the clear blue sky above. His eyes, hopeful and sad all at once, didn't blink. "Will you write me letters after I get home?"

"I'll write you," Sybaline said.

"We'll be pen pals," Nettle said.

"You can send us postcards from all the places you travel to and live. All the exciting places."

"I don't want exciting. I've had enough excitement to last my whole life." He cupped his hands around his eyes as he stared upward.

It was a fall day, and it was chilly out, despite the sunshine, but it was nowhere near so chilly as the bottom of the lake. Sybaline would never again question what it meant to be cold.

She would never question what it meant to be *herself*, either, or rather, if she did question it, she knew she would be brave enough to find all the right answers. Besides, she may not have magic any longer, but she had her family and friends, and most important, she had herself. She had her future.

As a family, they ate around the fire. They ate and told stories, laughing and screaming over every ridiculous thing that had happened beneath the lake.

A magical water wall rose! said Fisch.

We made the electricity work at home! said Nettle.

The sky started leaking, said Sybaline, though when she said it, it wasn't a part of the story she was proud of, because it also came with the telling of *Nettle collapsed* and *we had to figure out how to escape.*

The lake exploded! Aunt Ethel said, causing Momma and Auntie Wooline to shout and complain. Apparently when Sybaline broke apart the big bubble that surrounded town, she'd released all the air from it in one go. That air had shot through the lake, sending the surface up into a geyser, splashing the Lark family.

At the end of it all, they put out the flames to their fire and made their way into Cedric's borrowed truck.

Sybaline's bare feet squelched in the grass, and the bottom of her dress dripped water steady over her toes. She'd lost her boots somewhere in the lake as she'd floated to the surface. Walking away from the shore, she stepped back from both the valley and the lake, separating herself from the magic even farther.

The magic was its own living thing, like Benjamin had said. *The valley will be fine without us. The world doesn't need us, and the magic sure doesn't either. It's time for us to go and let the valley alone to take care of itself. Our fight's over now.*

He hadn't been quite right though. There had never been a fight for Sybaline to engage with, though she'd made one exist. She understood this now and understood too that in trying to save the valley and save herself, she'd almost killed both.

Sybaline took hold of Momma's hands and allowed herself to be helped into the bed of the truck. She climbed in and sat beside Nettle and Fisch. All they could do now was walk forward into whatever future awaited them. She, for one, might be scared of it, but she was also brave.

Brave and strong and no matter what, she could take her home with her wherever she chose to go.

ACKNOWLEDGMENTS

Nothing about this book was easy to write, but every part of it was rewarding and joyous.

When I moved from the middle of Appalachia in North Carolina back to my childhood home in Minnesota, I found it incredibly difficult to leave the place where I felt like I'd found myself. That move coincided with the time I was brainstorming the concept for *A Wilder Magic*. Looking back, I find quite a bit of myself snuck into Sybaline's story because of that move. Much of her journey mirrors mine: you can be both scared and brave at the same time, and making a home for yourself someplace new might be scary, but it's made easier when surrounded by those who love and support you.

There are *many* people who supported me while writing this book made it possible for me to tell Sybaline's story in an honest way. Thank you:

To Annie Berger, for giving me the space to write this book. This is one I desperately needed to write for myself, and I never would have done so without your encouragement. Sourcebooks is a beautiful home to have found. Thank you to everyone there who played a role in bringing this book to life: Cassie Gutman, Lynne Hartzer, Michelle Mayhall, Millie Liu, Nicole Hower, and Jordan Kost.

To Natalie Lakosil, for being my champion and being kindness incarnate when I send confused emails about publishing. You are truly an incredible agent.

To Mary Parton. I could never say thank you enough for inspiring the setting and history of this story. You gave me the avenue through which to write of my love for the mountains. Thank you for the endless days sharing your stories and wandering the hills, but mostly, thank you for being the soul-sister I desperately needed.

To Lacee Little, for being my go-to person, and the critique partner I can always trust with my vulnerable first drafts. You have gifted me so much wise advice over the last year. To Lauren Spieller, for helping figure out the ending of this story. My trip to visit you was invaluable, and I'm so grateful for the time we spent talking about our books.

To Jessica Vitalis, who pointed out the importance of acknowledging the history of the removal of Native Americans from Appalachia. Thank you for speaking up and showing me where I'd erred. To Rebecca Petruck. You are encouragement and faith personified. Thank you for not letting me write this book how I'd first imagined it. That was not the story I needed to tell.

To several readers for critiquing this book in a matter of days: Ash Van Otterloo, you lent me your Appalachian voice. Kurt Hartwig, you pointed out the overarching metaphors I was using without realizing it. Tara Creel, you encouraged me when I felt immensely unsure. Lorelei Savaryn, you provided support and a clear sounding board. You all devoted time and energy to this story; thank you.

To the communities in Appalachia who welcomed me so warmly: in Chattanooga, Tennessee, and in Sylva and Bryson City, North Carolina. I could never properly express my gratitude for accepting me so completely and for rooting me firmly in what it means to be from the mountains. An especially big thank-you to the kindergarten team at West Elementary who taught from 2015 to 2019: Gina Bradley, Liana Crisp, Amber Freshour, Hannah Farmer, Misty Teesateskie, Mary Ellen Helton, and Karen Parton.

And last, thank you to my family, for visiting me in all the places I have ever lived and for always providing a home for me to return to.

ABOUT THE AUTHOR

Juliana Brandt is an author and kindergarten teacher with a passion for storytelling that guides her in both of her jobs. She lives in her childhood home of Minnesota, and her writing is heavily influenced by her travels around the country and a decade of living in the South. When not working, she is usually exploring the great outdoors. She is also the author of *The Wolf of Cape Fen*. Find her online at julianalbrandt.com.